This could be the worst spring break ever—or just possibly the best.

❋

> *Dear God,*
>
> *I know you saw everything that happened today. Thanks for taking care of Tyler. But I'm a little upset about the trip. I mean, I know you don't always answer prayers the way I want, but didn't you hear how much I wanted to go on this trip? It's not my fault Tyler ran out in front of the car.*

She stopped typing, guilty that she was blaming her injured brother, who had cried his head off when he found out he couldn't go. And she was blaming God.

> *Sorry, that wasn't nice. But it would have been the best trip of my whole life. Oh, well, I guess Erin will have company at home now. Me.*

Tess saved the diary and turned off the computer, sitting silently, praying without saying anything really. Listening.

What about Erin? Maybe she could go with us! A smile spread across Tess's face like surf on sand. If her parents said yes, Tess wouldn't be alone, and the trip would be even more fabulous than ever.

Secret Sisters: (se´-krit sis´-terz) n. Two friends who choose each other to be everything a real sister should be: loyal and loving. They share with and help each other no matter what!

Secret ✳ Sisters

Holiday Hero

Sandra Byrd

WaterBrook
PRESS

HOLIDAY HERO
PUBLISHED BY WATERBROOK PRESS
5446 North Academy Boulevard, Suite 200
Colorado Springs, Colorado 80918
A division of Random House, Inc.

Scriptures in the Secret Sisters series are quoted from the
International Children's Bible, New Century Version,
copyright ©1986, 1988 by Word Publishing,
Dallas, Texas 75039. Used by permission.

The characters and events in this book are fictional,
and any resemblance to actual persons or events is coincidental.

ISBN 1-57856-114-0

Printed in the United States of America
1999—First Edition

10 9 8 7 6 5 4 3 2 1

To my "little" brother, Jeff Mike,
who was my childhood vacation buddy

one

Hit!

Friday Afternoon, March 21

"I'm sorry you have to stay home for spring break." Tess Thomas put her arm around her best friend and Secret Sister, Erin Janssen. "We would be staying home, too, if it weren't for my mom's business trip."

The two girls leaned against the wall of Coronado Elementary School, waiting for Erin's mom to pick her up. The late afternoon grew hotter as they talked. Tess fingered her short, brown, bobbed hair, letting the breeze whisper against her neck. Arizona warmth washed over her. Spring bloomed everywhere; tiny daisies struggled from the ground looking like miniature fried eggs.

"Tell me all the details," Erin said with a sigh. "I'll try not to be too jealous. But it'll be hard."

"Well, the shoe company she writes ads for is having its annual convention in San Diego at the Hotel del Coronado. Royalty and movie stars stay there and everything. Our whole family is going." Tess stared into space, dreaming about the trip.

7

"And?" Erin asked.

"She only has to work a couple of hours each day, so we're going to Sea World and the Wild Animal Park. And, of course, we'll be right on the beach."

"Send me a postcard every day," Erin said. "I'll just be sitting here, bored, watching TV. I don't even have any good books to read."

"Say there!" Eight-year-old Tyler rounded a sun-scrubbed corner of the school, walking up to where the girls stood. Tess's little brother often spoke in a British accent, preparing for a career as a Scotland Yard detective. "Dashed difficult waiting here for you, old girl. I'm eager to prepare for the vacation of my life! I have to pack, and then I have to take Hercules over to Big Al's and get all my reptile reference books ready. Let's be off!"

"I told you five minutes ago I'm waiting until Erin's mom picks her up." Tess put her backpack on the pinkish gray gravel. "It'll only be a few minutes. Hercules, the horned toad wonder, can wait. Besides, aren't you afraid Big Al will kill him while you're gone?" Tess ran her hand over his dark brown cowlick. She knew it bugged him.

"You don't have to wait with me, Tess," Erin interjected.

"I want to! We're going to be apart for a whole week. Tyler can wait. He's just excited about the trip." Tess smiled. "Can't say I blame him."

"Don't be such a pill, old fruit. Big Al will take swell care of Hercules. He knows that, next to Al, Hercules is the most important friend I have." Tyler glanced at his watch. "You know, I'm jolly well old enough to walk home by myself."

"You're not allowed to cross this street without me. It's way too busy! You know that. I'll only be a minute," Tess said.

Tyler rolled his eyes before walking away a few feet to talk with Big Al.

Mrs. Janssen pulled up in front of the school.

"Have a great time. I'll miss you," Erin said with a smile that Tess thought seemed forced.

"I'll see you at church Sunday." Tess hugged her. "But I'll miss you, too. And I'll bring you back something."

Erin smiled again, then climbed in the car, and her mother pulled into the street.

Tess turned toward Tyler and Big Al. "Tyler, I'm ready. Let's go." She saw Big Al but not Tyler. Where was he? She scanned the courtyard but didn't see him. He couldn't have started home by himself—could he? No, he would never disobey their parents like that.

"Oh, no!" Blood rushed to her head, and her heart pounded double time. She saw Tyler walking between two parked cars, looking down at his Game Boy rather than watching the traffic.

"Tyler!" Tess screamed. The screeching brakes from an oncoming car sent a smoky cloud of burnt rubber over the schoolyard. The car spun completely around, slamming against the curb.

Someone screamed, "Call the principal!"

Then she saw Tyler lying in the road, motionless.

two

Close Call

Friday Afternoon, March 21

"Tyler! Tyler!" Tess finally forced her legs to move and raced to the street. She knelt beside Tyler and touched his face, which was clammy and cool. Her own fingers were frozen with fear. She stroked his cheek. His eyes opened.

"What am I doing here? What happened?" he asked.

"Don't worry. You're going to be okay." Tess squeezed back the tears. The pebbles in the road bit deeply into her knees, but she ignored the pain. A minute later Erin and Mrs. Janssen ran up beside her. A crowd gathered around.

In what seemed like hours, but Tess knew had been minutes, the off-and-on wail of a siren grew closer, finally stopping next to them.

Two medics jumped out. "Here we are, young man," one of them said. After carefully probing for neck and back injuries, the men slid Tyler onto the stretcher. Tess scrambled into the back of the ambulance after them.

"Just a minute, young lady. I'm afraid you can't ride back here," a medic said, putting a hand on Tess to stop her.

"But he's my brother! I can't let him go alone!" Tess said.

"He'll be all right. Can someone here take care of you?" The driver looked around, and Mrs. Janssen stepped forward.

"We'll follow in our car," she said. "The principal has called their mother. She's on her way to Scottsdale Memorial North."

The ambulance whisked Tyler away. Trembling, Tess climbed into the Suburban with Mrs. Janssen and Erin. Erin held Tess's hand, and Mrs. Janssen prayed aloud, with her eyes on the road. "Lord, we pray for your protection and healing on Tyler, that your hand would be upon him. Allow the doctors to help him right away. Lessen his pain, Jesus, and let him be all right. Thank you. Amen."

Tess sighed. Her parents weren't Christians; they wouldn't be praying. But Tess was a Christian, and she knew that prayer was what Tyler needed most.

"I feel so bad," Tess said. "I should have walked home with him when he asked."

"Don't blame yourself," Mrs. Janssen said. "He was crossing a very busy street. It's not your fault."

Tess turned to look out the window, willing the blocks to fly by faster. Every light was red, to Tess's frustration, but in minutes they arrived.

Tess jumped out and ran into the emergency room. Her mother was already there, sitting in a brown vinyl seat.

"Mom," Tess fell into her mother's arms. "Is he going to be all right? Is he going to die?"

Her mother stroked Tess's hair. "No, he's not going to die. But what happened?"

"I told him to wait for me to walk home; it was only going to be a few minutes," Tess explained. "But he went without me, and now look. He just should have listened to me and everything would have been all right. But now it's not!"

Her mother shook her head. "That's why I make rules. I wish you guys understood that rules are meant to keep you safe."

"I understand, Mom. It's not like I broke any rules!"

"You're right." Her mother squeezed Tess's hand. Mrs. Thomas stood up, holding her hand against the small of her back.

"Does your back hurt again?" Tess asked.

"It's all right, honey. Now that I'm almost six months pregnant, the baby weighs more, and it strains my back a bit. It's okay," she reassured.

"Does Dad know about Tyler?" Tess said. "What's going to happen to our trip to San Diego?"

"Dad's on his way," her mother said, ignoring the question about the trip.

I guess it is a little selfish to worry about that now, Tess admitted to herself.

At that minute a young doctor in a green scrub suit snapped his clipboard shut and approached Tess and her mother. "We've done some X rays. We're waiting for them to develop. My guess is that he fractured his left leg. I'm sure there's no internal swelling or bleeding. He's a very lucky young man."

"So he's all right?" Mrs. Thomas asked.

"Yes, yes, he'll recover just fine. But for a few days he will have pain, and then he has several months of recovery ahead of him."

"Will he need to stay overnight?" Tess's mom asked.

"I don't think so, but I'll make that decision after I see the developed x-rays. I'll send a nurse to escort you to him as soon as he's back from radiology. Then I'll consult with you when I've seen the film." He snapped open his clipboard and went into a curtain-drawn compartment to check on another patient.

Then Tess remembered Erin and her mother. Looking around, Tess saw them sitting quietly in the waiting room. She went to Erin's side, and Tess's mother followed.

"Will he be all right, Molly?" Mrs. Janssen asked Tess's mom.

"Yes. They think his leg is fractured, but that's all." She dug through her purse, looking for a tissue.

"Here." Erin's mother handed her one from her own purse.

"Thank you," Mrs. Thomas said shakily. "And thank you for bringing Tess."

"Oh, it's nothing at all."

Just then Tess's father strode through the automatic doors and headed toward his wife. "How is he?" His brows were furrowed, and his normally smooth face was creased with worry.

"He's going to be okay," Mrs. Thomas said, allowing her husband to fold her into his arms.

A nurse arrived and said, "You may see your son now."

"Oh, thank you!" Mrs. Thomas said.

"We'll leave. Please call if there's anything we can do." Mrs. Janssen put her arm around Erin and led her toward the door.

"Call me tonight," Erin whispered to her friend, squeezing her hand one last time.

"Okay." Tess felt better now that she knew Tyler was going to be okay.

The three of them walked into the cubicle where Tyler lay on an examining table. His skin was the color of sticky Chinese rice, white with a little gray shadow. Even his lips looked orangish blue, not pink. Tess could see her mother was struggling not to cry as she kissed both of his cheeks.

"How are ya, buddy?" His dad walked up to him.

"I'm sorry, Dad," Tyler said.

"I know you are. Don't worry about it. The most important thing is that you're going to be okay."

Tyler struggled to sit up a little, but his dad gently placed his hand on his forehead. "Don't move, buddy."

"Can I still go to San Diego?" Tyler said. "Can I, Dad? Can I? I already have the film loaded for the reptile pavilion at the zoo, and I've saved three pages in my scrapbook for all the postcards I'm going to buy. Did you know I saved up my allowance? I didn't spend even one cent so I could buy a movie at the reptile house." Tyler struggled to sit up again, his brown eyes pleading. "I'm not going to miss that, am I? Please say I can still go."

Mr. and Mrs. Thomas looked at one another.

"Let's wait to see what the doctor says, honey," Mrs. Thomas said.

"Okay." Tyler smiled a little. "I'm going to close my eyes."

Tess bit her lip. Tiny blue veins like spiders' webs crisscrossed his eyelids.

A minute later the doctor reappeared.

"Tess, would you buy me a soda from the machine in the waiting room?" her father asked, handing her a dollar.

"Sure," Tess said.

As she walked to the soda machine, she prayed in her head, *Lord, thank you for rescuing Tyler. Thank you, Jesus, that he is going to be okay and not die. God, please make him not hurt too much or feel too bad. He's just a little kid, and even though he's a pest, I love him.*

She fed the dollar into the machine and punched the largest red button. The can clattered to the bottom, and she whispered one final plea, *Please, please let us be able to go to San Diego, Lord. Don't say he can't go. Did you hear him, God? Did you hear how much he wants to go?* She finished praying, certain God had heard.

three

Hey, What About...

Friday Night, March 21

A couple of hours later they drove home. Tess squeezed into the front seat with her parents so Tyler could stretch comfortably across the backseat.

"Ouch!" he said each time the car hit a bump, even though their dad drove slowly. A few minutes later, Mr. Thomas opened the garage door. Dinner sounded really good to Tess.

"Can we order a pizza?" she asked as she walked into the house, tossing her denim jacket on a hook inside the door.

"Yeah, pizza," Tyler said, his voice sleepy from the pain medication. His father carried Tyler into his bedroom, their mother running ahead to pull down the covers. Tyler still had the hospital gown on.

"I think you can use those for pajamas tonight," his mother said.

Tess peeked at them. After tucking Tyler in, her dad set Hercules' cage next to Tyler's bed.

"Tess," Mrs. Thomas said with a sigh, "would you order the pizza?"

"Okay," Tess said, but as she left, she listened a bit while her parents talked, sitting on either side of Tyler's bed.

Don't eavesdrop! a voice whispered inside her heart. Tess's parents had forbidden her to eavesdrop on other people's conversations. But it wasn't really disobeying if she bent down to take off her shoes, right? Then she just couldn't help overhearing.

"I'm sorry, honey, you won't be able to go." Mom's sooth-ing voice carried across the hallway.

"No, Mom!" Tyler broke out in sobs. "I want to go. I've been waiting and planning. There's no zoo by us with that many reptiles. And they have all those special books and stuff. What about Shark Encounter at Sea World?" He cried even louder.

"I wish I had never gone to school," he continued. "I wish Tess would have gone home when I asked her. It's all her fault!" He cried into his pillow.

It's not my fault! Tess thought. *He could have waited.* Deep inside, though, a prick of guilt poked her conscience. She could have gone when he asked. She knew how excited he had been. After tossing her shoes down the hall, she went to order the pizza.

She called, then raced up the hall when her parents left Tyler's room, closing the door behind them.

"You said we could talk about San Diego when we got home. So we're home. What's the deal? Are we going?"

"I want to rest a minute, Tess." Her mom walked into the family room and tossed the newspaper off the couch before lying down. "Go change your clothes, and we'll talk about it over pizza."

"Yeah, but—"

"Tess, you heard your mother. Now!" Her father pointed toward her room. His jaw muscle flexed, and Tess knew it was useless to argue.

She sighed as she slipped her dad's old sweatshirt over her head and pulled on a baggy pair of fleece pants. It felt like being wrapped in a big, warm blanket. She plopped tummy first onto her bed. Under the pillow was the book she had been reading, *San Diego with Kids*. Dog-eared pages marked places she wanted to go. Would she ever get there?

She must have dozed off because she was startled awake by her dad tapping on her door. "Pizza's here," he called.

Shakily, she sat up. *Oh, gross.* A thread of drool trickled from the side of her lips. She wiped it on the back of her shirtsleeve before pushing the sleeve above her elbow. Swiveling her full-length mirror, she glanced at herself. *Double gross.* "I'm coming," she called, heading into the kitchen.

"So," she said as soon as she settled into her seat and had eagerly bitten into a piece of deep-dish-with-everything, "Whf bot da twrp?"

"Could you swallow and try it again?" her mother suggested.

"What about the trip?"

Her father glanced at her mother, then spoke. "The doctor said it would be better for Tyler to stay in bed for a few days, maybe a week."

"Oh no!" Tess dropped the pizza. "He must be totally sad!"

"He cried for a good long time after we told him," Mrs. Thomas said.

Poor Tyler! He was more psyched for this trip than I am. A terrible thought crept into her mind. She blurted it out. "Does that mean I can't go either?"

"Well, I don't know if anyone is going," her mother said, setting down her own piece of pizza.

"Now, Molly, you know you need to go. We can't afford for you to offend these guys and lose the account, especially with the baby coming. Besides, aren't you receiving an award?"

"Yes, Jim, I know the account's important. And so is the award ceremony. But what about Tyler? He's more important than any stupid shoe account."

Tess looked up. Her mother never said *stupid*.

"The doctor said he'll be just fine, good as new. There's no risk to his health anymore; the bone will set, and there's no bleeding. He'll be okay. I'd never let you go if I thought there would be any problem," her father said.

"Oh, I know, but there's just something about a mom being there," she replied.

"You can call every day. I'll put the television in his room, and we'll watch sports and play Game Boy and eat chips and dip. It won't be the same as the trip would have been, but I can make sure he'll have a good time. I can handle it." Mr. Thomas reached across the table and touched his wife's hand. "Now eat," he said, and she picked up her piece of pizza again.

"Well, what about me? Can I still go?" Tess said. "I mean, I'm not injured, you know? I'd be good company."

"Honey, I just don't think that's possible. I'll be working several hours a day, and I can't leave you alone in the hotel."

"Oh, great. So I have to stay home the entire spring break and watch ESPN with Tyler and Dad. How much fun can one girl have?"

"I know it's disappointing," her dad said. "But we can rent some movies and stuff. And you can go over to Erin's house. I'm sure you two will think of something great to do. You always do."

"Yeah, but Dad, this is spring break! I don't want to do something I already do on normal days. It's not like I disobeyed or anything. Tyler's the one who broke the rule, and I'm getting punished for it. Is that fair?" She sat with her head in her hands. "I'm going to my room for a while."

"Don't you want any more pizza?"

"No, I'm not hungry." Tess dragged herself from the kitchen to her room. After closing her door, she booted up her computer and loaded her diary program.

The icon flickered, and she typed her heart out.

Dear God,

I know you saw everything that happened today. Thanks for taking care of Tyler. But I'm a little upset about the trip. I mean, I know you don't always answer prayers the way I want, but didn't you hear how much I wanted to go on this trip? It's not my fault Tyler ran out in front of the car.

She stopped typing, guilty that she was blaming her injured brother, who had cried his head off when he found out he couldn't go. And she was blaming God.

Sorry, that wasn't nice. But it would have been the best trip of my whole life. Oh, well, I guess Erin will have company at home now. Me.

Tess saved the diary and turned off the computer, sitting silently, praying without saying anything really. Listening.

What about Erin? Maybe she could go with us! A smile spread across Tess's face like surf on sand.

If her parents said yes, Tess wouldn't be alone, and the trip would be even more fabulous than ever. Almost leaping off the bed, she ran back to the kitchen to tell her parents this wonderful plan. But she closed her eyes when she passed Tyler's room. He would feel even worse if her plan came true.

four

The Call

Friday Night, March 21

"I know, I know; I have the solution!" Tess skidded into the kitchen in her stocking feet.

"What is it?" her mother said with a smile.

"How about if Erin comes with us? You know, then I wouldn't be alone, and she wouldn't be sitting here by herself. Dad and Tyler can watch all the sports they want and stuff."

Eyes sparkling, Tess sat down and grabbed a fresh piece of pizza, tearing into the crust while waiting for her parents' response.

"Well, I don't know, Tess. I mean, I don't need to have two twelve-year-olds sitting alone in the hotel while I'm working any more than I need to have one. In fact, it would be worse. I'd be responsible for someone else's child."

"Please, Mom, we would be just fine. I promise. We would do whatever you told us. Then, when you're done working, we could go to Sea World and the Animal Park and everything. I know it's the solution." Tess sounded confident but inside she was pleading. Couldn't her mom see how perfect this was?

Tess plunged on. "I'll find something totally fabulous— amazing even—and buy it for Tyler while we're there. I'll take all the pictures he wants, *and* I'll buy him whatever he wants from the reptile pavilion. Tons of stuff. So he won't feel too bad about being left out." She popped open a soda. The seconds ticked away. No one said anything. Tess's enthusiasm fizzled like the bubbles in her Coke. Her parents were going to say no. Great.

"What if Erin's mother came, too?" Dad suggested. "I don't even know if she could, but that might work. She could supervise you two while Mom is working, and then the four of you could go off and sightsee. It would be someone to share the driving with, Molly. I have to admit, that was one thing I worried about: your doing all the driving. But this would solve that problem, too."

"Well, maybe. If she could be gone five days. Do they have other plans?"

"Nope, they're staying home," Tess said with a grin.

"Where would the boys stay when Ned Janssen was at work?" Mom asked.

"Well, since Erin's dad is a chef, he works evenings," Tess said. "Maybe their grandma and grandpa could come over. They only live in Gilbert. It'll be like a girls' trip, Mom. I mean, just the four of us."

"Yes, that might be fun. And we won't have another chance to do this before the baby is born in July. It just might work." Her mother picked at a hard piece of mozzarella on the cardboard box while she talked as much to herself as to Tess.

"And I do like Nancy. I wouldn't mind spending some time with her. Okay. Give Erin a call. Tell her we would be driving over Monday morning and coming back Friday night. If Erin wants to go—"

"If Erin wants to go!" Tess interrupted. "Of course she does! Are you kidding?"

"If Erin wants to go," her mother repeated firmly, "she can talk about it with her mother. Then have her mom call me."

"Thank you, Mom. This is the best day of my life. I mean, I wish Tyler were going, but since he's not, this is sooo good." A speck of guilt buzzed around her like a pesky fly. Poor Tyler. She swatted it away. What could be done now? She promised herself she would buy him something incredible in San Diego. And he did bring this on himself, right?

Tess kissed her mom and dad and ran to her room to make what she knew was the best phone call in Erin's life.

five

A Dream Come True

Monday Morning, March 24

Tess's dad loaded their stuff into the car. Tyler stared out of his bedroom window. It was open, and Tess could hear him crying.

Should I go talk with him? She walked back into the house and into his room.

"I'm really sorry, Ty," she said, meaning it. "We've always been vacation buddies."

"I...I know," he said between little, mouselike sobs. "I wish I'd never tried to walk home by myself." In her head, Tess agreed. If he had obeyed her, he would be going with them today. He wasn't old enough to make his own decisions. But she said nothing, knowing it would just make him cry harder. Instead, she scooted next to him. "I promise I'll find you some really great stuff."

"Please look all over the zoo for reptile stuff," Tyler said. "Look for anything Hercules might like. And maybe a movie. And if they have any cool books." Tyler sat back against his pillow, the low drone of the TV in the background.

"I will," Tess promised. She would find him great stuff even if she did nothing else on this trip. Well, she would have fun, too. But she would make his stuff her priority.

After giving him a hug, she walked back outside to kiss her dad good-bye before she and her mom pulled out into the wakening day.

A few minutes later, the Thomas's Jeep drove up in front of Erin's house, and Tess's mother turned off the engine.

"I'll see if they're ready." Tess jumped out and rang the doorbell.

"Hi, Tess." Tom, Erin's fourteen-year-old brother, opened the door. For a minute Tess didn't know what to say. He was looking even, um, older. And cuter.

"Hi, Tom," she finally choked out. The tile in front of Erin's house wasn't really all that fascinating, but she stared down at it anyway.

"It's really nice of you to invite my mom and sister to come with you. How come you didn't invite me?"

Tess looked up but didn't answer. What could she say to that?

"I'm just kidding," he said. "Come in." Tess stepped in as Erin lugged a suitcase and her backpack down the hallway. Tess helped her out to the car. A minute later Erin's mom followed, and before the dew had completely melted into the ground, they were on their way.

An hour or so later the long expanse of desert stretched before them. Tess watched the Jeep vacuum the road underneath it, endless white lines and all. Long-armed saguaro cacti waved one-handed good-byes as they traveled from Phoenix through west Arizona toward San Diego.

"How is Tyler doing?" Erin's mom asked. "We've been praying for him."

"You have? Thanks." Tess's mother looked genuinely pleased. "He's doing really well. He'll be just fine. Remind me to call him when we stop for lunch, will you?" A shadow crossed her face, and Tess knew her mom was wondering if she should have come at all.

"You should see his cast," Tess broke in. "It's light blue with planet stickers all over it. He wanted a rain forest, but they didn't have one."

"Want some?" Erin shook a box at Tess.

"What are they?"

"Frosted Nerds."

"Breakfast of champions? No thanks." Leaning toward her best friend she whispered, "At least they're the only nerds on this trip. Wouldn't it have been awful if we both had to stay home?"

"Yes!" Erin breathed a sigh of relief. "Thanks so much for asking me. This is my best spring break ever!" She reached into her backpack. "And because you asked me, you are my hero." She swooned, faking a geeky smile. "My Holiday Hero."

"You geek." Tess giggled.

"I brought something else for my Holiday Hero. Do you want it?" Erin pulled out a blue and yellow box of Lemon Heads, Mr. Lemon winking at Tess.

"Now here is the real breakfast of champions!" Tess said, shaking a few into her hand. After a couple of minutes, Tess dozed off, and she was surprised when her mother announced they were stopping for an early lunch.

"Already? How far have we gone?" Tess rubbed the cloudiness from her eyes, trying to focus.

"Pretty far. We have less than two hours left," her mom answered. "And I'm hungry. Eating for two, you know." She patted her bulging tummy.

"I'm starting to worry you're not going to fit behind the wheel," Tess teased.

"Now see here, young lady, I'm not getting that big." Her mother gently tugged a piece of Tess's hair.

"I know," Tess answered.

She and Erin walked in ahead of their mothers, Tess clutching the $20 bill her mother had handed her.

"Order for me, too," her mom said. "Cheeseburger, fries, and water. I need a pit stop in the rest room. Then I'm calling home."

"I'll take the same," Erin's mother said. "And I'll find us a table."

"Let's pretend we're sisters when we order," Erin suggested.

"Who's pretending? We are sisters!"

Before Tess reached the counter, she wondered what drink to order. She wanted a Coke, but her mom usually said only one soda with caffeine per week. She had had a Coke with her pizza just the other night. Well, it wouldn't be the same rules for now. Vacation was different. And her mother hadn't said anything so it must be okay. She ordered a Coke.

A greasy, teenaged boy wiped his hands on his apron and grinned a creepy smile. He took their money. "I'll bring it over when the hamburgers are up."

The girls sat down with Mrs. Janssen.

"Tess?" Erin said.

"Yeah?"

"Well, talking about your mom's tummy reminded me. What if you get a real sister." Neither Tess nor Erin had sisters. They had chosen each other to be best friends and sisters of the heart.

"What do you mean?"

"I mean, if this baby is a girl, you won't need me for a Secret Sister. And my mom isn't having any more kids. So I'll be the only one without a sister." Erin fidgeted with her shoelace, not looking at Tess.

"Erin, I'll always be your Secret Sister. Forever. Even if the baby is a girl, which it probably isn't since it's so big already. Nothing will ever change between us."

Erin smiled, looking her friend in the face. "You just want my Lemon Heads," she said.

Tess laughed, and the greasy teenager walked up just ahead of Tess's mother. "Here's your order, girls," he said. No one mentioned the Coke.

An hour or so later, on the road, Mrs. Janssen asked, "May I put in a CD?"

"Sure," Tess's mother answered. Mrs. Janssen slipped it in, and Erin winked at Tess. It was a Christian music group.

"List time." Tess whipped out a notepad.

"What?" her mother asked.

"List time. Of what we want to do. To make sure we get to do everything we want. I mean, this is a dream come true. We can't miss out!" Tess rolled a Lemon Head around in her mouth, puckering as the sour coating sizzled on her tongue.

"Well, put down Sea World," her mother said, "and the zoo."

"Don't forget beach combing," Erin's mom said.

"And buying a great gift for Tyler." Tess wrote "Cool Gift—Tyler" on her pad. "Was he okay when you called, Mom?"

"Yes. Still very sad, I'm afraid. Dad said he doesn't want to watch TV or even play Nintendo." Her mother blinked back the tears. Tess felt some welling in her eyes, too. Not want to play Nintendo! The Thomases didn't have a player of their own, so Mom had rented one for Tyler this week as a special treat. And now he didn't want to play?

"I'm sorry he missed the trip," Erin said.

"Me, too." Tess said.

As Tess spoke, her mom drove onto a long, wide bridge spanning the bay between San Diego and Coronado. Tess and Erin rolled down their windows and looked out over the glistening water, awestruck. A fishy smell wafted in, and the girls breathed deeply of the ocean air. As soon as they pulled off the bridge, they passed a large, beautiful building with cascades of cherry red bougainvillea tumbling in rich bouquets.

"Is that the hotel?" Erin asked.

"No, that's a house," Tess's mother answered with a smile.

"A house?" Tess said as both girls gasped. "Wow."

"Let's see who can guess which is our hotel," Erin suggested. Minutes later they turned down Orange Avenue and drove toward the hotel. Tess spotted it first, looming on the horizon like a fairy tale.

"There it is, isn't it, Mom?" she said.

"Yes."

"It looks like a frosted wedding cake!" Tess said, awestruck at the swirls of white paint. "With a gingerbread roof." The car slowed down, and shouts of laughter rolled up the beach as Tess watched masses of children at play.

Erin dropped her Frosted Nerds to squeeze Tess's hand. "It's a dream come true."

six

Bomb Scare

Monday Afternoon, March 24

"May I park your car, ma'am?" A uniformed valet opened Tess's mother's car door, and another valet opened Mrs. Janssen's. Then they opened Tess's and Erin's doors.

"Yes," Mrs. Thomas answered. "The name is Thomas." The valet handed her a ticket, and she began to walk toward the hotel.

"Mom, what about the suitcases?" Tess whispered, glancing over her shoulder at the Jeep.

"They'll deliver them to the room."

"How will they know where we are?"

"The front desk will tell them."

"Cool!" Erin whispered to Tess.

They approached the curved stairway in the hotel and walked into a plush, richly carpeted lobby.

"Man, can you believe it?" Erin asked. A large chandelier hung in the center of the room, each piece of crystal sparkling like a dewdrop reflecting the sun.

"Look over there." Tess pointed to a gold cage elevator

with a man inside. "What's he doing?" she asked her mother.

"He operates the elevator. We need to get in the check-in line," her mother said. Tess looked around while they waited.

"Why is that crown there?" Tess pointed to the ceiling where a lighted crown was centered.

"'Cause *Coronado* means 'crown' in Spanish, remember?" Erin reminded her.

"Oh yeah. Well, now we can have our own Coronado Club," Tess giggled, referring to the in-crowd at their school.

"Yeah, and ours is better," Erin agreed.

While Tess's mom registered them, Tess, Erin, and Erin's mother hung back from the front desk. But Tess overheard the conversation.

"I'm here to check in," Tess's mom said. "The name is Thomas."

"Certainly. Welcome to the Hotel del Coronado." The neatly uniformed woman spoke with an Australian accent.

"Doesn't that sound cool?" Erin whispered. "I wish I had an accent."

"Me, too," Tess agreed.

Minutes passed, and Mrs. Thomas shifted from foot to foot, then stretched her back.

"I'm sorry, ma'am. We don't have a reservation for Thomas. I've checked everywhere. Do you have a confirmation slip?"

"No, I don't. But I'm here with the shoe convention. Do you have other reservations, or are they all lost?" Mrs. Thomas snapped.

Great. Mom is freaking out with the front-desk clerk. Total embarrassment. And now we have no room. I knew this trip was too good to be true. Maybe this is punishment for taking the trip when Tyler couldn't. There won't be a room, and we'll have to turn around and drive home. God, please don't let that happen.

"Yes, of course we have other reservations," the clerk answered calmly.

"I think they were planning to make reservations for me," Mrs. Thomas said in a clipped voice.

"Actually, it appears most of the others made their own reservations," the clerk explained. "I'm sorry." Tess watched her mother's face pale from pink to chalk.

"Oh," she said quietly. "I thought they were making them for me. And they must have thought I was doing it. How silly of me."

"It's all right," the clerk said with a smile. "I'll see what I can find for you." She turned to the computer, and Tess heard her mother clear her throat.

"I'm sorry I lost my temper," Mrs. Thomas said. "I'm tired from the drive."

"Understandable." The clerk smiled again. She was a lot nicer than Tess would have been if someone had just bitten off her head.

"You're in luck. I've found something for you. It's one of our nicest rooms, with an ocean view. We've had a cancellation today, so I can give it to you for the convention rate."

Yes! Tess's heart leaped. *An ocean view. Could this get any better?*

"Thank you," Tess's mom said.

The four of them walked through the Palm Court, then outside, and finally into a small circle of rooms. Mrs. Thomas opened the door to their room.

"Ta-da!" she said.

"Fantastic!" Erin flopped on one of the beds. Tess flopped on another one. Amazing.

"I said a silent prayer when they couldn't find our room," Erin whispered.

"Me, too," Tess said. "We must have been praying at the same time!"

Erin walked into one of the two bathrooms, then came back out. "Look!" She held up a little basket of soaps, sea salts, and lotions. "Can we use them?"

"Yes," Mrs. Thomas said. Then she turned her back as she dialed the phone. Probably calling Tyler again. Tess pushed the guilt away.

Mrs. Janssen pulled back the wispy white curtains, and they all gazed out over the open ocean.

"Dreamy," Tess said. "Let's go out on our porch." The porch swept around the entire room. Four white wicker rocking chairs waited patiently in the late afternoon sun.

"Unpack first," her mother said, and Erin's mother nodded her agreement.

Soon they had unpacked everything except Mrs. Thomas's briefcase. She tossed it into a closet. "I'll have to worry about work soon enough." Tess grabbed her camera as they walked outside.

"When is the awards ceremony, Mom?" Tess smiled proudly. The company was honoring her mother for writing the most effective ad last year.

"Thursday afternoon," her mother answered.

"Can I come and watch?"

"No, I'm sorry, honey. Kids aren't allowed. But I'll tell

you all about it." Her mother drew up a chair. They all sat down.

Salty air caressed Tess, and she turned her face toward the sea. The wind was as cool as fresh sheets, gently blowing gauzy clouds through the sky. She shut her eyes and rocked back and forth like the swaying waves.

"Look!" Erin said.

Tess opened her eyes and saw Erin pointing to something in the water. "What is it?"

"Dolphins, I think!"

"Or maybe whales," Tess said. She snapped some pictures for Tyler's scrapbook. He liked whales.

"Maybe." Erin looked doubtful. "I like dolphins better though."

"Me, too," Tess agreed. She tilted her head toward the open window to their room, which was right behind them. A strange, muffled beeping came from somewhere inside the room. "What's that noise?"

"What noise?" Mrs. Janssen asked.

"That beeping. Can't you hear it?"

They all perked their ears a bit, and soon Tess's mother agreed. "I can hear it, although it's faint. We'd better check it out." She walked into the room. The others followed.

"I can still hear it, but I can't locate it," her mother said. "It's not beeping very often." She opened the closet doors and listened. "I thought it came from here, but now I don't hear anything. No smoke detector is in this closet, or anything else I can figure."

After at least five minutes of searching, they were all confused. Tess was getting a little scared. "What if it's a bomb?"

"A bomb! Tess, why would a bomb be in here?" her mother asked.

"I don't know. You said famous people came here. Maybe a spy planted it and that's why the people cancelled their reservations."

Her mother frowned, but Tess saw that her mom at least thought it was a possibility.

"Well, I'm not going to make any more wild guesses. I'm calling the front desk." Mrs. Thomas picked up the phone and explained the situation before setting down the receiver.

"Security will be here in a minute," she said.

Erin looked at Tess, who looked back, eyes wide open.

seven

Making Plans

Monday Night, March 24

The knock on the door came within minutes. "May I help you with something?" A maintenance man stepped in as Mrs. Thomas opened the door. She explained the beeping noise; then the four of them stepped to one side to wait.

No one spoke. He walked into the closet, listening closely. When he emerged, he held the briefcase. "Ma'am, I think you'll find the beeping noise is coming from this case." Seconds later another muffled noise bleated, clearly from the briefcase this time.

Blushing, Mrs. Thomas unzipped the case. After digging, she located her voice recorder. "Oh no!" She sank into the chair, red-faced. "Somehow during the trip the 'Play' button switched on and wore down the batteries. The beeping noise was the low battery indicator."

"This is so embarrassing," Tess whispered to Erin as Mrs. Janssen thanked him and shut the door. "First she wigs out at the desk, now this!"

"Well, I'm glad that's all it was," her mother said, clearly flustered.

"Don't worry about it," Erin's mother said. "It just adds excitement to the vacation."

"Anyone else hungry?" Erin asked hopefully.

"Yes, I am," Tess's mom said. The others agreed.

They walked outside, through the twilight to the Prince of Wales Grill. Tyler would have loved this place. The restaurant overlooked the ocean, and the napkins were all folded in patterns. Tess couldn't snap a picture, but she promised herself she would write down everything about it, and then he could paste the paper in his scrapbook. Satisfied that she was doing her best for her brother, she ate a hearty dinner before they returned to their room.

"I want to plan our day tomorrow," Tess said. "Let's go to the zoo first. I want to make sure we buy Tyler's presents right away so when I call him I can tell him we got them. Then maybe he'll feel like playing Nintendo."

"I need to work in the morning," her mother said. "I'm not sure for how long. Why don't you girls swim in the pool?"

"I'd like to take a tennis lesson," Mrs. Janssen chimed in.

"Good idea. Then when I've finished for the day, we'll go to the zoo."

"Why is the zoo so cool?" Erin asked.

Tess opened her travel book. "Look here! It's the biggest zoo in the world!" She pointed out pictures of double-decker bus tours, soaring gondola rides over the park, and hands-on activities.

Erin glanced at the brochure. "Ooh, that does look fun.

Especially the gondola ride with my Holiday Hero!" Erin sat up. "Can I take a bath with those sea salts?"

"Sure," her mother answered. Erin opened the closet she and her mother shared and pulled a thick terrycloth robe off a wooden hanger. She draped it over her arm and twisted her hair back with her free hand. "I'll be back after my beauty bath." She batted her eyelashes as Tess rolled her eyes in amusement. Erin was a goofball, but she was Tess's best friend.

Mrs. Janssen strolled onto the veranda for a while to watch the evening sea and to stargaze. Tess's mother called home, and after talking to Tess's dad and Tyler in a low voice, she hung up.

"Oh, Tess, I'm sorry. I was so preoccupied with Tyler that I didn't think to ask if you wanted to talk with him."

"It's okay, Mom," Tess said. "I'd rather talk with him tomorrow night, when I can tell him about all the pictures I took at the reptile house. And the cool stuff I bought."

Her mom handed a thick manila envelope to Tess. "Here's something Tyler sent for you," she said. "He put it together yesterday, and just now he reminded me to give it to you."

"What is it?"

"He didn't tell me. I'm going to make a call to check on my schedule tomorrow; then I'll be in the other bathroom taking out my contacts." Her mother picked up her notebook and walked toward the living-area phone.

Tess ripped open the top of the large beige envelope and pulled out a note. It was written on a lined piece of notebook paper in Tyler's neat block printing. Tess would recognize it anywhere.

"SISTER DEAR, I JOLLY WELL AM UPSET THAT I CAN'T BE THERE WITH YOU HAVING FUN, BUT IT'S NOBODY'S FAULT BUT MY OWN." Tess swallowed a lump in her throat. Having Erin here was fun, but she wished Tyler could be here, too. They always shared vacations together. And he had been looking forward to this trip so much. She kept reading.

"I FIGURED, DASH IT ALL! WHO WILL BE THERE TO BUG YOU? I PLANNED TO BRING MY BIG BOOK OF DISGUSTING FACTS WITH ME AND SHARE SOME TIDBITS DURING THE TRIP. HI HO, CAN'T BE THERE NOW. SO I'VE WRITTEN SOME THINGS DOWN AND PUT THEM IN ENVELOPES. ONLY OPEN A COUPLE A DAY, THE ANIMAL ONES WHEN YOU GO TO THE ZOO, YOU GET THE IDEA. HAVE A GOOD TIME, GOOD ENOUGH FOR BOTH OF US, OLD FRUIT. THANKS. TYLER."

Tess folded the notebook paper and slipped it into her Bible. She didn't feel better; she felt worse. Guilt crept under her collar, fanning heat onto her face. But it wasn't her fault he couldn't be here. If he had obeyed her, none of this would have happened. She didn't break his leg. He just wasn't old enough to know when he had to obey and when he didn't really have to. Right?

She grabbed the stack of smaller envelopes stashed inside the large one. On the face of one of them was written, "#1. OPEN AFTER DINNER." She tore it open, and a note card fell out.

Scribbled on the front was, "WHY DID TESS TOSS PEANUT BUTTER INTO THE OCEAN?" Turning the card over she read, "TO CATCH A JELLYFISH." Smiling in spite of herself, she tucked the card into her Bible with the note. She shuffled through the envelopes again and read the fronts. Some said, "READ AFTER THE ZOO." A couple said, "SEA WORLD."

She came to the last envelope. "OPEN WHEN YOU SEE THE BEACH." She tore it open. The card read, "WHY WAS THE OCEAN ARRESTED? BECAUSE IT BEAT UPON THE SHORE. DON'T GET INTO ANY TROUBLE, OLD GIRL." Tess giggled. Trouble? What kind of trouble could she get into here? Poor Tyler. She would definitely look for something cool to buy him at the zoo tomorrow.

After putting on her pajamas, she sat down to wait for Erin. Tess opened her Bible and read a few verses. Then she heard a knock at the door. She opened it. Nobody there? All of a sudden some boys walked by.

Just then she remembered her pajamas. Tess slammed the door and breathed a sigh of relief. They couldn't have seen her. At least she thought they hadn't seen her. And even if they had, she would never see them again.

"What are you doing?" Mrs. Janssen asked Tess. Erin emerged from the steamy bathroom bundled in the extra-large robe.

"Nothing. I thought I heard a knock," Tess answered. She walked over to Erin. "I was almost embarrassed to death. I'll tell you later," she whispered.

"It was probably me closing the patio door," Erin's mother said. "My turn for the bath." She headed toward the bathroom she and Erin shared.

After Erin put on her pajamas, she and Tess sat cross-legged on Tess's bed and talked. "I can't wait for tomorrow," Erin said. "It's going to be a total blast."

Tess smiled. "Me either. I'm too excited to sleep!"

eight

Danger!

Tuesday, March 25

The morning broke bright and sunny, just as a vacation day should.

As Erin's mother laced up her tennis shoes, she told the girls, "Molly and I decided you can swim and shop the gallery, but you can't leave the hotel grounds." She coughed.

"Are you okay?" Erin asked her mother.

"Just a little cough," her mom said.

"Okay." Erin turned toward Tess. "Ready?" She pulled some sweats over her swimsuit.

"Let's go! Vacation, here we come!" Tess said. She grabbed her fanny pack and room key and out they went.

"Let's swim first," Tess said. "Then our hair can dry while we're looking at the shops."

"Okay." The pool was a short stroll away, so they cut through the video-game room.

"Erin," Tess whispered as they entered the room, "I think those are the two boys I saw." She glanced over toward the pinball machine.

One boy played the game, shaking the machine like a geek, trying to make the pinging ball score some extra points.

"Oh no!" Tess whispered. "It *is* them!"

"Them who?" Erin looked confused.

"The pajama guys. I mean, the guys who might have seen me in my pajamas," Tess whispered. "Let's get out of here!"

Before they could make a quick escape, the boy with the brown baseball cap stepped into their path, blocking the door. "Hey, isn't that the girl we saw having a pajama party last night?" he said to his friend.

Oh no! Death, come quickly! He saw me after all! Tess ducked her head.

"Oh yeah. So it is. I hope she's not wearing pajamas to the pool," the freckly one teased. Tess peeked at him and saw his smile. The girls kept their heads low and practically ran from the room.

"Oh, Tess, can you believe it?"

"No, I can't. And I am *not* going to take off my sweats and let those geeks make fun of me in a swimsuit!" Tess rolled her towel into a pillow, then hopped onto a white vinyl lawn chair to stretch out.

Erin did the same. "Well, maybe they'll go away. Even though the one in the brown hat is sort of cute."

"You are impossible. Whose side are you on?" Tess giggled. "Let's wait them out." Instead of going away, though, the boys came to swim.

"Come on in, it's warm!" they called, swimming close to the edge near Tess and Erin. Then they splashed as hard as they could.

"I didn't know it was kiddie aerobics this morning," Erin said loudly as a glob of water landed on her head.

The brown-haired boy just smiled and splashed her some more. "Want to join our class?"

"I think he likes you," Tess whispered.

"I think he's a cheese ball!" Erin said. "Let's get out of here." The girls walked up the stairs toward the shopping gallery.

"Bye, girls. See you later!" the freckly one called.

"Not if I can help it," Tess muttered, but she was smiling. He wasn't Tom, Erin's brother, but he was sort of friendly looking. "Let's see if they have anything in these stores for Tyler."

"Sure," Erin said. "I might even buy some postcards myself."

An hour or so later they were back at the room. Mrs. Janssen was waiting for them. After they told her about the bothersome boys, they discussed their shopping expedition.

"There was nothing much for Tyler," Tess said.

"The postcards were cool though." Erin tossed hers onto her bed.

Just then the door opened. "Okay, girls, let's go." Tess's mom said as soon as she entered the room. "I've worked hard all morning, and now I'm ready to play!"

"Yippee!" Tess said. "We're dying of boredom."

"There are always those boys to talk with, if you're that bored," Erin's mother teased.

"I'd have to stop breathing for about an hour before I'd be bored enough to talk with them," Erin said. "Do you have the camera?"

"Yep," her mom answered.

"Then let's go!" Mrs. Thomas said.

They drove the short distance to the San Diego Zoo.

After they paid their entrance fees, Tess scanned the park. "I want to take the bus tour first," she said, pointing toward the loading dock for the double-decker tour bus.

"Let's sit on the top," Erin suggested.

"Of course." Erin's mom said. They all climbed to the top.

"Whoa!" exclaimed Tess as the bus took off in a cloud of greasy diesel smoke. The vehicle shimmied and shook and seemed about to plop over on its side. "Whose idea was this anyway?" Soon, though, she settled down and started to snap pictures of the giant bears. Leathery elephants paraded next to the bus.

"Look, there's the rhinoceros!" Erin called. Sure enough, a huge, horned creature lumbered over near the bus, twirling her ears like pinwheels. Their bus driver explained that the mother rhino had been pregnant for two years.

"Aren't you glad you're not a rhino?" Tess asked her mother.

"I feel like one sometimes." Her mother giggled, patting her large stomach. "But, yes, nine months of waiting for this baby will be just enough. Three months to go!"

Tyler, Tess reminded herself. *Can't forget about the gift.* After the gondola they would hit the reptile section, and then she would spend a good, long time in the gift shop. She would buy lots of lizard stuff, just like he wanted.

The bus ride was over too soon. They walked around the park for another couple of hours, then Mrs. Thomas said, "Let's eat, and then you girls can ride the gondola. I don't think my tummy can take it, and Nancy said she'll stay with me."

After a hamburger and cherry icee, the girls boarded the bright yellow gondola buckets.

"Keep your hands inside and don't stand up!" Tess's mother called after them.

Tess rolled her eyes as the gondola headed skyward with a jerking motion.

"Cool," Erin said. The gondola climbed higher and higher. "I wish they had other rides."

"Maybe they will at Sea World," Tess said. "Hey, are those gorillas down there?" She leaned over the side.

"Tess, don't lean over. I mean, I like wild rides, but I'm not crazy."

"I want to see those gorillas. We didn't get to see them from the bus."

"You can't see anything from up here. We'll check it out when we stop."

"No," Tess said. "It'll take too long to walk over there. I'll just look from here." She stood up in the gondola, sending it swaying.

"We're not supposed to stand up!" Erin pleaded.

Tess leaned over the side. "Oh, don't be such a goody-goody. I know what I'm doing."

"Your mom said to sit down."

"Don't you think I know how to be careful? I'll sit down in a second." The bucket swayed again. Tess grasped for the side of the gondola to keep her balance, slamming her wrist against the metal. The force unclasped her silver charm bracelet. It was just like Erin's, and they always wore them as a reminder of their friendship.

The bracelet fell off and caught on a hook on the outside

of the gondola. It swung in the wind, threatening to drop to the ground.

"Can you reach it before it falls?" Erin asked. "Should I help?"

"No! That might tip over the cart," Tess said. "I'll lean out and try to grab it."

"Don't," Erin begged. "You'll fall out and be killed."

"I have to get it!" Tess said. She stretched her arm as far as she could. Just then, the gondola lurched again.

"Tess!" Erin screamed.

nine

After All

Tuesday Afternoon and Evening, March 25

Tess fell back into the gondola as the ride smoothed out. She opened her fist. Inside was her bracelet.

"Oh, you got it!" Erin said. The gondola jerked into port, and they jumped out. The attendant eyeballed them but didn't say anything. Maybe he hadn't seen the close call.

Tears trembled in Tess's eyes, but she willed them not to fall in public. Why did she want to cry now that the worst was over?

"Do you want to visit any more animals?" she asked, her voice shaky, teeth chattering with fear.

"No," Erin said. "I just want to go back and get our moms."

"Me, too," Tess said. She didn't say anything else, but her heart ran wild. She had almost fallen. Even Erin didn't know how close she had come to losing her balance. And breaking her neck.

They climbed into another gondola bucket for the return trip.

"I guess I'll stay seated this time," Tess said, not sure if she was trying to make a joke or not.

"Yeah," Erin said. "And keep your arms in." They both broke out in nervous giggles.

Tess fastened the bracelet back on her arm. No more crazy stunts, especially not for something silly like a gorilla. *Thank you, God,* she prayed, *for saving my bracelet. And my life.*

Later that night they strolled across the street from the hotel to eat at a tiny Mexican restaurant. On the walls hung thick, colorful rugs, and tiny red lights twinkled from the ceiling.

Soon the waitress served their meals.

"Mmm, this is good!" Tess slurped a strawberry freeze through a straw.

"I don't know why you girls want Mexican food. We can have that every day at home," Mrs. Janssen said.

"Because it's good!" Erin answered, cheese dripping from her enchilada. "Did you bring those envelopes from Tyler?"

"Tyler!" Tess said. "Oh no!"

"What?" Mrs. Thomas looked up. "What about him?"

"I forgot to go to the reptile house today—and the gift shop!" Tess pushed away her plate. Her stomach sank as she remembered why she had forgotten. If only she hadn't had that close call on the gondola.

"Oh well, I'm sure we'll find something nice somewhere else. Maybe at Sea World," her mom said.

"But it won't be the same!" Tess wailed. Nothing would be the same. "He wanted reptile stuff." She had only one small thing to do for her brother while she was here, and now she had blown it.

"I think I saw a specialty pet store near the top of Orange Avenue," Mrs. Janssen said. "We'll check it out tomorrow. Did you bring the envelopes from Tyler?"

Tess fished them out of her fanny pack.

"Well, read one," Erin said.

"Okay. 'HOW DOES A GIRAFFE CLEAN ITS EYEBALLS AND EARS?'" Tess flipped the card over and giggled while waiting for the others to guess.

"I don't know. With sticks in the trees?" her mom offered.

"No, Mom. Anyone else have a guess?"

Erin and her mother shook their heads so Tess blurted out, "'With its twenty-inch-long tongue!' And he wrote right here, 'THIS IS ABSOLUTELY TRUE. I DIDN'T MAKE IT UP.'"

"Ooh, disgusting," Erin said. "I'm still eating, you know."

"Gross," Mrs. Janssen agreed. Then, with a smile in her eyes, she said, "Are there any more cards?"

"Yep." Tess opened the second of three. "This one says, 'I HOPE YOU LIKED THOSE CUTE LITTLE KANGAROOS WITH THE BABIES IN THEIR POUCHES.'"

"Now what's he going to say about the kangaroos. They were adorable!" Erin said, scooping up spicy red sauce on a hot tortilla chip and popping it into her mouth.

"'THEY'RE RELATED TO RATS.'" Tess giggled.

"Ooh, gross." Erin said.

"Okay, last one," Tess said. "Eew," she said reading it to herself. "Do you guys remember that big smelly water buffalo?"

"Yep," her mom said. "What about it?"

"They use its milk to make mozzarella cheese."

"Oh, gross," Erin's mother said.

Erin asked, "Pizza, anyone?"

"Eew," they all chimed at once.

"I'm bushed!" Mrs. Thomas said. "And I have to work tomorrow before Sea World. My comfy jammies are calling to me."

They strolled back across busy Orange Avenue and walked into their room.

"We're not tired yet," Tess said. She flipped open her Bible and stuffed tonight's three note cards in. She would read her Bible tonight, too.

"Watch some TV," her mom suggested.

"Bo-ring," Tess responded.

"Well, I suppose you can walk around the hotel grounds for a half-hour. But no going out by the ocean, and you absolutely can't leave the hotel grounds. Do you want me to wait to call Tyler?"

"Uh, no." Tess shifted from foot to foot uncomfortably. "I'd rather call him tomorrow when I can tell him I bought him something cool."

"Okay," her mom said.

Tess and Erin walked across the glittering courtyard toward the hotel shops. In the evening twilight the hotel looked even more beautiful. Tess stopped dead in her tracks.

"What?" Erin asked. "I don't like that look, Tess." A shadow crossed Erin's brow.

"Well, I was thinking that maybe we could just head back to Orange Avenue and see if we could find that pet store."

"We're not supposed to leave the hotel, remember?" Erin asked. "Maybe we'll find something for him at Sea World tomorrow."

"Hmm. Could be," Tess said. But she wasn't sure at all.

ten

The Promise

Tuesday Night, March 25

Tess decided to obey and not leave the hotel grounds—for now. Later that night she sat by herself on the porch outside of their hotel room, rocking slowly in a white wicker chair. She drank in the slow sound of the surf foaming on the beach then retreating to the depths. The hotel lights brightened the evening enough so she could read her Bible. But they didn't dim the stars' glimmer as they sparkled in the inky night sky. The moon cast a shimmering shadow on the water, and in the distance red and green lights twinkled on the sterns of fishing boats anchored till dawn.

"What a cool world you've made, Lord," she said with a sigh, opening her Bible. "Crumb, I forgot my Sunday school lesson." She thumbed through her Bible, looking for the paper she had to fill out by church next week. "I guess I won't read my Bible tonight then."

Do you need a lesson to hear from God? Startled by the thought, she decided maybe she would read some, after all. But where?

She had stuck Tyler's cards in the Bible just anywhere, not wanting to lose them. But now she opened up to a page in which she had stuck the ones from tonight. Ephesians 6. Might as well start at the beginning of the chapter.

"Children, obey your parents the way the Lord wants. This is the right thing to do. The command says, 'Honor your father and mother.' This is the first command that has a promise with it. The promise is: 'Then everything will be well with you, and you will have a long life on the earth.'"

Tess snapped shut her Bible. *Boy, isn't that the truth? I mean, if Tyler had obeyed, he would be here right now instead of lying in bed at home. And everything would have been well with him. But that can't be helped now.*

Standing up, she stretched and fingered her nearly lost bracelet. Thank heavens she had retrieved it. *All's well that ends well, right? Better head to bed. Tomorrow, Sea World!*

eleven

Half a Brain

Wednesday Afternoon, March 26

Early the next afternoon they arrived at the huge Sea World parking lot.

"I am so psyched to be here!" Erin said. "I wouldn't mind being a marine biologist when I grow up."

"I thought you wanted to be a vet," Tess said.

"Well, yeah, but marine biologist would be cool, too. Think about it, swimming with dolphins, diving for coral. Where should we go first?"

"How about the dolphin show?" Mrs. Thomas suggested. "I think we should do all the things we really want first. Then, if we run out of time, we've covered the highlights."

"Sounds great," Erin said. She consulted the schedule. "The next dolphin show starts in half an hour, so we better find some seats now." Tucking the map back into her pocket, she led the way to the dolphin stadium.

"Let's sit in the splash zone!" Tess said. The first fifteen seats were marked as a place where the audience was certain to get drenched.

"No way!" both mothers said at once.

"You two can sit there," Erin's mother said. "As for me, I'm planning to stay high and dry."

"We better go with them," Erin whispered. "I see snack sellers walking around, and I don't want to spend my own money on treats."

Erin and her food.

They settled down in a middle row of shining silver bleachers, which were out of the splash zone, and munched on popcorn. Tess's mom bought two giant Shamu cups brimming with ice cubes and lemonade. The girls slurped the drinks while waiting for the show. The sky was a thin blue, and the sun baked them, even in March.

Tess pushed her hair back from her eyes, hoping to get a little tan. Maybe she could have spring-break brown skin by the time she got home.

"Look, they're ready to start," Erin said. Sure enough, wet-suited trainers came out and introduced the "stars," seven adorable dolphins. Their smooth, gray skin shone in the sun, and their high-pitched voices squeaked sweetly and gently.

"What a dream job," Erin said with a sigh. The dolphins raced around the stadium, tossing rings back and forth, cruising with their trainers on their backs around the huge, bright pool.

"I like Dolly Dolphin best," Erin said. "Maybe we can get dolphin posters and make them into book covers."

"Yeah, to cover some awful book. Like Health," Tess agreed. The show ended when one brave audience member walked to the pool's edge to work with the dolphins. And of course, in the end, one of the more playful ones splashed with all her might, drenching the poor guy.

"I hope he brought more clothes." Erin giggled and tossed the empty popcorn container into the garbage on the way out.

"Look," Mrs. Thomas pointed. "Caricature artists. Let's have them draw your pictures."

"Oh Mom!" Tess said with a groan.

"Now, Tess, I haven't asked you for much on this trip. I'd really like to have them."

"Okay." She wouldn't admit it, but it might be kind of fun.

She and Erin sat in black-backed director's chairs, side by side. A college-aged art student picked up a pen and colored chalk and quickly drew pictures of the girls.

Please, Lord, don't let him draw huge ears. Why do my ears have to be so big?

He didn't draw the ears. But he did draw the girls on two dolphins' backs, riding a wave in the pool.

"Cool," Erin said as she examined the completed work. Tess had to admit it was a great souvenir of their vacation together.

"Shall we visit the Shark Encounter?" Erin's mother asked.

They wandered through the shark pool exhibit, making faces at the fierce, ugly sharks that swam circles around the tank. One tiny rock pool cupped baby sharks no longer than a finger.

"Aren't they cute?" Tess tapped the glass nearby.

"You always go for the babies," Erin observed. "But they are cute. Until they grow up, that is."

"Same with human babies," Tess's mother teased.

"Seriously, it's hard to imagine how something so small

and simple can grow into such a killer," Tess said, moving forward. Tyler had really wanted to come to the shark exhibit. He had planned for weeks to snap pictures of the sharks, to read all the signs about them. He had even watched a National Geographic movie on sharks over and over, wanting to learn all he could. And now he wasn't here. And he wasn't even playing Nintendo. He was sitting at home, all alone, in the dark probably.

The crowd was starting to crush her, and Tess wanted to get out so she could breathe easier. She made her way outside, hoping to spy a shark gift shop.

She didn't see one right away, but she did spot something she wanted. A few minutes later she and Erin pulled long tufts off the huge cotton candy they had bought. The treats were swirls of pink and blue sugar clouds wrapped around a white paper cone.

"Look, I'm Colonel Sanders!" Erin joked. Tess laughed. Erin did sort of look like the Kentucky Fried Chicken guy when she held a piece of fluff under her nose as a fake mustache.

"You goof." Tess elbowed her.

"Oh, could we please feed the dolphins?" Erin asked.

"Sure," Tess's mother said.

They strolled over to the hands-on exhibit, and Tess and Erin each bought two little cartons of smelly fish. Erin held hers close to her chest, but Tess stuck hers out at arm's length.

"Pee-yew!" Tess said, holding the fish away from her. "This stuff stinks." Before she knew what was happening, a flock of sea gulls swarmed out of nowhere and started to peck at her fish. They stabbed their long beaks into her carton, tossing the fish down their throats as fast as they could gulp.

"Help!" Tess said, dropping the almost empty carton to the ground. The sea gulls gobbled up the last of the fish and went to find another victim.

"Oh no!' she said. "All my fish are gone." She looked around to see if anyone had seen her panic. She didn't want to look like a weirdo.

"You can share mine. " Erin offered one of her cartons to Tess.

Just as Tess was about to grab it, a Sea World employee came forward. "We saw what happened."

Great. Who else saw?

"We replace any fish the sea gulls steal." He handed her two new cartons of dead fish. "Be careful this time!"

Tess thanked him, and she and Erin moved to the edge of the dolphin exhibit. Tyler would have laughed his head off if he had seen the bird attack. She would have to be sure to remember to tell him about it tonight.

"Here, fishy, fishy," Tess called. She looked at the flat, dead eyes of the fish. "How could any creature think this is appetizing?"

"Good thing *you* don't want to be a marine biologist," Erin teased. She took one of the slimy fish and flopped it into the pool by its limp tail. In no time at all a dolphin swam up, poked its head out of the water, and opened its mouth.

"Cute! Doesn't it look like it's smiling?" Tess asked. Rows of tiny white teeth lined bright pink gums. Tess tossed one of her fish into the dolphin's mouth.

"Do you think it's a boy or a girl?" Tess asked.

"A girl," Erin answered.

Amazed, Tess said, "How do you know?"

"Because it's cute, that's how." Erin giggled. "Look, here comes her best friend. Maybe they're sisters like us." Tess tossed a fish into the "sister's" mouth, and Erin fed the first one. Soon they were out of fish and washed the goo off their hands.

A short time later, tired from the sun and fun, they headed back to the van and then the hotel.

"I brought one of Tyler's envelopes," Tess said, ripping open one that said, "READ AFTER SEA WORLD." She read aloud, "DID YOU KNOW DOLPHINS NEVER SLEEP? HALF OF THEIR BRAIN SLEEPS AT ONE TIME, THEN THE OTHER HALF. HEY, TESS, MAYBE YOU'RE A DOLPHIN SINCE YOU ONLY USE HALF YOUR BRAIN!"

She shook her head, giggling. Then it hit her. Maybe she did have half a brain. She had forgotten something very important—again.

twelve

Orange Avenue

Thursday, March 27

The next morning started badly.

"I'm sorry, girls, I feel awful." Mrs. Janssen dropped her head back onto the pillow. Her face looked drawn. "When I woke up, I felt okay. Molly said I looked feverish, but I didn't think about it. She left, and now I feel awful! I'm sorry, but I don't think I can take you shopping."

"Do you want me to stay here with you, Mom?" Erin said.

"No, honey, but thanks. I'm just going to sleep and hope this goes away."

"Okay," Erin said. "We can spend some time at the pool this morning." "Yeah," Tess said, but her face dropped. This was awful! She felt bad for Erin's mom, but what about Tyler? Now that she had blown her chances of buying him something at Sea World, she needed to shop Orange Avenue.

"It must be the flu. Oh, why didn't I get a flu shot?" Mrs. Janssen mumbled. "Why don't you girls meet back here in a couple of hours?"

"Can we eat lunch at the deli next to the pool?" Tess asked.

"Yes." Mrs. Janssen closed her eyes. She fell back against her pillow again, and soft whooshes of air escaped as her head sank in.

Tess and Erin slipped out the door, putting the "Do Not Disturb" sign on the knob.

A couple of minutes later Erin stopped. "I forgot my earplugs."

"Do you really need them?" Tess asked.

"Yeah, I get ear infections," Erin said. "C'mon, let's run back and find them."

They headed back toward the room, but as they approached it, they noticed the sign on the door had been flipped over. Now it read, "Please Make Up This Room."

"Hey, maybe your mom is feeling better!" Tess cheered up.

"Mom?" Erin called softly, clicking open the door. Soft snores came from the bed.

"Doesn't look like she has moved." Erin grabbed her earplugs from the desk and walked back toward Tess.

"How could the sign have flipped?" Tess closed the door. After turning it over again, they walked back to the pool.

"Hey, Jack, over here!" She heard someone whisper in a hallway. The urgency of the whispered voice stopped the girls in their tracks.

"Here's another one," the voice said. Two boyish giggles burst out.

Erin led the way. She and Tess peeked around the corner. Tess caught sight of a brown cap and a red head. The boys had flipped all the "Do Not Disturb" signs to "Please Make Up This Room." Unknowingly, the maids might enter rooms where people were sleeping or dressing.

"Uh-oh," the brown cap said, looking at Tess and Erin. "Looks like trouble."

All four stared at one another for a long minute. No one said a word. Then the boys ran off.

"Ha!" Tess said. "I have a feeling they won't bug us anymore. Or we'll have this little incident to hold over their heads."

"Right!" Erin agreed. "Looks like we're in for a peaceful morning swimming." She was right. The pool was cool and empty with only a whisper of wind blowing over the day.

After swimming the girls visited Windsor Chocolates. The little candy store, tucked into a cute corner of the hotel, was stocked floor to ceiling with every kind of sweet treat a person could want.

"I've never stayed in a hotel that had its own candy store," Erin said.

"Me neither. It's great!" Tess opened up a plastic bag and chose candies from the large, clear bins. She tossed in some coated sour licorice. Sky-colored sugar crystals clung fast to the outside of the intense raspberry licorice. Her mouth would be bright blue after eating it, but who cared. It tasted so good. Next she scooped up black and white gummy sharks and some candy corns.

"You like those?" Erin asked.

"Yeah, why?"

"I think they look like dirty teeth. You know, pointy and all yellow and orange."

"Gee, thanks," Tess said. "I guess I won't be eating those anymore now that you grossed me out for good!"

Erin scooped a rainbow of jellybeans and sour cherry licorice into her bag. She peered into a back bin. "Swizzle sticks!"

"I want one, too," Tess said. Erin reached in, handing back several wooden sticks coated in sweet pink, purple, and emerald green jewels.

"Why don't you buy Tyler something from here?" Erin braided two twist ties around her plastic bag. It barely closed, bulging to the point of popping.

"I could, I guess. It's just that, you know, he can get candy at home." Tess twisted her bag shut, too.

Erin nodded. "Well, I'll bet my mom is feeling better. Let's get burgers at the deli for lunch; then we can go back to the room and change. I know you can find something cool for him on Orange Avenue. Like at the exotic pet shop up the road."

"Yeah," Tess agreed, smiling. "That's just what I'm thinking, too."

An hour or so later Tess's plans crashed. Mrs. Janssen was still in bed, pale with cold sweat soaking the bedsheets. Tess's mom came back to the room for just a second.

"I'm sorry, Tess, but today's the award ceremony, and I can't leave early. It should be over by about 5:30." Mrs. Thomas reapplied her lipstick and dabbed a little clear nail polish on her nylons.

"Why are you doing that?" Tess watched her.

"There's a run. If I dab it with nail polish, it won't run all the way down my leg. It's my only pair so I need to make them last." Her mother slipped her feet into her shoes.

"But, Mom, the shops close by dinnertime!" Tess had overheard someone saying something like that.

"Well, Tess, I'll try my best. But Erin's mom needs to stay in bed, and you guys need to do something by yourselves today." Her mother kissed her cheek. Tess rubbed off the lipstick mark.

"I'll be back as soon as I can. You girls meet me here at 5:30, and we'll see what we can do." She grabbed her brief-case and walked out the door.

The sisters walked over to the video room, but Tess spied the two boys in there.

"Forget it!" Tess said, turning away. "I'm not in the mood to deal with them." She sat down on a sculptured concrete bench near the tennis courts.

"I thought you said the redhead was sort of cute," Erin said. "It might be fun to play some pinball with them."

"Yeah, well, maybe if I had already bought Tyler's stuff. But get serious! It's the last day we're here. I messed up at both the zoo and at Sea World. I can't even bring myself to talk with him on the phone."

"Didn't your mom say he played with his Nintendo last night?" Erin asked.

"Yeah, but I bet he was just trying to make her feel better. I know he is counting on me to buy him some reptile stuff. I can't let him down." Tess bolted up. "You know, I think it would be okay to shop by ourselves for a while."

"We already shopped every store in the gallery," Erin said, pulling a thread out of her shorts.

"Not the gallery," Tess said. "Orange Avenue."

"We're not supposed to leave the hotel," Erin said. She stopped picking at her shorts and looked Tess in the eye.

"I know. But it's not like we're babies who are going to run into the street or anything. Every decision I've made has turned out just fine. It's not our fault your mom is sick and mine has to work."

"Well, that's true," Erin said. She pulled the thread all the way out of her shorts and worked on another. "We could get in big trouble. Why not wait till tomorrow?"

"'Cause we're going home tomorrow. My mom is in a big hurry to get back to Tyler. I doubt she'll shop at all. And then I won't have anything to give him!" Her mind wrestled with twisting thoughts. She could get in trouble. But she hadn't yet. And it's not like she was a baby who couldn't decide what was good and what wasn't. It couldn't really hurt, could it? "They didn't tell us not to go on Orange Avenue today, only to stay off the beach. And we will do that."

"I guess it might be all right, since you're doing it for your brother. I mean, that's not really a selfish reason," Erin slowly said.

"Right," Tess said. "And it'll save them from having to shop." She pushed back the wave of doubt crashing on her heart and smothered the voice that whispered, *No*. She must buy something for Tyler. Today.

Tess stood up and locked her fanny pack around her waist. "Let's go."

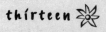

thirteen

The Bus

Thursday Afternoon, March 27

"I can't believe we haven't found that pet store." Tess kept trudging down the street, disappointed again. "It seems like we've been walking forever."

"We have been." Erin dragged behind her. "Are you sure that pet store is on this street? Are you sure you can't buy him something else?"

"I don't know if it's on this street," Tess snapped. "But your mom said it was. And no, I can't buy him something else. The reptile stuff is what he really wants, what he's been waiting for. Since he couldn't come, I wanted to make sure he at least got what he wanted." They sat down on a bench outside one of the shops.

"I'm thirsty. Want a drink?" Erin asked.

"Yeah," Tess's voice softened. After all, this wasn't Erin's fault.

"I'll bet there's some place to buy a drink up the road a little. I thought I saw a bagel shop."

The two girls wandered up the sidewalk another half block.

"I guess I'll just buy him something at home. Maybe get a subscription to *Reptile Magazine*."

"He'd probably like that," Erin said. But her voice sounded unconvinced, and Tess wasn't sure either. Wasn't the whole point to buy him something he couldn't get at home? She should have done it at the zoo. Why, oh why, had she forgotten?

They walked into the bagel shop and stood in line.

"Tess!" Erin elbowed her.

"What?" Startled by the jostle, Tess moved aside.

"Look! The clock! It's 5:20, and we're supposed to be back at the hotel room in ten minutes!"

The girls ran from the shop without purchasing their drinks. Tess scanned the long, long street stretching between them and the hotel.

"We'll never make it," she said. "We're doomed."

"I told you we shouldn't have come," Erin said. "Now we're in for it for sure."

"Nobody dragged you," Tess said. "Besides, you looked like you were having a good enough time shopping." They started to walk fast, almost running down the road. In her heart, Tess knew it was useless. They had at least two miles to cover.

They sat on another bench, catching their breath. "I suppose we could call," Erin said.

"Yeah. Do you have any change?"

"I think so." Erin dug through her fanny pack, tossing out gum wrappers and a used tissue.

Tess looked up at the pole next to the bench. She read the words "Bus Stop" just as a bus pulled up.

"Erin, get the change out!"

"Why, what are we doing?" Erin stumbled as Tess pulled her to her feet. The bus belched a gust of gas and stopped.

"We'll take the bus. We'll hop off right in front of the hotel and get there just in time."

"Aren't we in enough trouble without taking a bus, too?"

"Don't be a baby. I'm trying to get us out of trouble, not in more trouble. Come on!"

The girls walked up the steps and fed their coins into the meter. As soon as they were on, the doors slammed behind them with a menacing, final thud.

fourteen

Full Speed Ahead!

Late Afternoon, March 27

"Where should we sit?" Erin whispered as the bus jerked into gear. They smelled more than saw the oily black smoke burp from the exhaust.

Tess considered the options. One seat was open to the left, but the guy next to it smelled as if he hadn't showered since the Civil War. To the right was a body-pierced beauty rocking out to something on a portable CD player.

A kindly, chubby grandmother scooted over on her bench, leaving two spaces. She moved her shopping bag to the floor and pulled tight her cotton sweater.

"Thank you," Erin said and elbowed Tess as she sat down.

"Yeah, thanks," Tess said. The granny nodded but said nothing.

With fierce concentration Tess looked out the window. Where was the hotel? It couldn't be too far. Why, oh why, had her mother had to work late? If she could have come home earlier, this wouldn't have happened.

It couldn't be too far now. "How do you let them know when you want to get off?" she whispered to Erin.

"I don't know." They looked around. Strung across the top of the seat was a long cord connected to a bell by the driver's seat. "I think you pull that," Erin said, fidgeting in her seat.

"Yeah, that's right. I remember now," Tess said. Had she ever been on a bus? Or had she just seen it in the movies? She couldn't remember. But the cord thing sounded good to her. Just as she was about to hold onto the cord so she would be ready when they came close to the hotel, she heard Erin gasp.

"Oh, oh," Erin said. "I just dropped my five-dollar bill!"

Tess looked down. "I'll help you find it." She knelt on the bus's dirty floor and reached way back under the bench.

"Ooh, disgusting!" Erin said. She bent over and watched as Tess navigated her hand around cigarette butts and spitty gum. Spying the bill, she grabbed it just as it was about to flutter down the aisle.

"I got it!" Tess cried, then jumped back up onto her seat.

"Oh good," Erin said. She looked out the window. "Oh bad."

"What? What is it now?" Tess asked. Did Erin always have to find the bad?

"We just raced past the hotel," Erin said.

Quickly Tess looked out the window. Sure enough, the Hotel del Coronado was growing smaller and smaller behind them as they drove away. A small squiggle of fear, like the tiniest spider, crawled up her backbone as she realized their trouble was growing with every turn of the bus's tires.

As if to make it worse, the bus driver stepped on the gas. They flew down the freeway toward the lonelier beaches and away from town into the deepening twilight.

fifteen

First Prayer

Thursday Evening, March 27

"Tess, I'm scared." Erin huddled close to her Secret Sister.

"Me, too," Tess whispered back. Now what should they do? What if this was a bus to Mexico or something? After all, Mexico was only a few miles away. What if they crossed the border and couldn't get back?

"Should we ask the old lady?" Tess whispered, glancing out the window as the sun set over the sleepy Pacific Ocean. Above the water the sky swirled gauzy clouds. The sinking sun dyed them pink and blue, and they looked just like the cotton candy at Sea World. Had that been only yesterday? It seemed like a million years ago.

"Isn't that like talking to strangers?" Erin asked.

Tess nodded. She guessed it was. Even the kind-looking old lady next to them could be a murderer or something. After a minute or two, Tess spoke again. "I guess we should just pull the cord and see where he lets us off."

"What if he stops right in the middle of the road? Should we walk?"

"I don't know. But I don't know what else to try either."

Erin nodded her approval, and Tess reached above her head and gave the grimy cord a hard yank. A tinny "ding" rang out next to the bus driver. The girls sat forward in their seats, tense now, waiting to see what happened next.

What will my mom think? Tess wondered. Her mother had enough trouble worrying about Tyler, and now this. If Tess were lost forever, her mother would be devastated.

"What are you thinking about?" Erin asked.

"My mom," Tess said.

"Me, too," Erin admitted. "What if my mom gets sicker when she realizes I've disappeared?" Her face went gray.

Within a few minutes the driver steered the bus to the side of the road, kicking up a bit of gravel as he overshot the edge. Applying light pressure on the brakes, he slowed the bus to a stop and finally cranked open the doors.

"I guess we get off here," Tess whispered, standing up. Erin grabbed her fanny pack, and on unsteady legs they wobbled toward the front.

The chubby granny spread out over their now vacant seats.

Soon the girls were left alone in front of Silver Strand Beach. A beautiful stretch of blond sand tickled with gold shimmered in front of them.

"Any other time I'd be so psyched to be here," Tess said, scanning up and down the deserted stretch of beach. "With parents," she added. A beige brick bathhouse rested near the ocean.

Erin saw it, too. "Maybe a phone is over there," she suggested.

"We're not supposed to go near the beach, remember?" Tess said.

"Well, now's a good time to decide to follow the rules," Erin snapped. Turning her back toward Tess, she stomped across the thin highway to a bus bench on the other side.

Reluctantly, Tess followed her toward the lonely bench. It sat astride a clump of blooming weeds. Just beyond the bench Tess noticed what seemed to be a military building. And guard gates. She sank down next to Erin.

"What's that supposed to mean?" she asked. "About following the rules?"

"Well, if you had obeyed and stayed at the hotel, none of this would have happened," Erin said. She looked near tears.

"I don't remember your refusing to go. And you followed me on the bus, too." Tess said. *Why did she have to bring that up now? As if I don't feel bad enough already.*

The night crept closer, tiptoeing silently up the beach and across the street. It grew darker and colder. Lonely noises, like lapping waves and a train whining in the distance, covered the space between the girls.

"What should we do?" Erin asked.

"Well…" Tess thought for a minute. "I can't believe I didn't think of this sooner, with all the mess we're in. But we've never prayed together before. I mean, we've prayed separately, and in Sunday school and everything, but not together."

Erin perked up. "That's true. And just think about the day we checked in. We prayed at the same time but not together. And look how great that worked out. Let's try it." She held out her hands to Tess, who took them in her own.

"Erin," Tess said.

"Yeah?" Erin opened her eyes, surprised. She must have been expecting a prayer.

"I'm sorry I got you in this big mess."

"It's okay." Erin squeezed Tess's hands. "You're right. I could have said no and refused to go. But I didn't."

A cool breeze caressed their hair, and Erin bowed her head. Tess stared at Erin's lowered head for a minute before bowing her own. Erin looked like a flower bending in the shore-swept wind.

"God, I'm really sorry," Tess started. "I made some bad choices here and disobeyed. I guess...I guess I thought I was old enough to make my own decisions." Tess stopped praying for a moment, as Tuesday night's Bible verse popped into her mind: *Children, obey your parents the way the Lord wants. This is the right thing to do. The command says, "Honor your father and mother....Then everything will be well with you."*

"You're right, God, I hadn't even thought I'd memorized that verse, but I guess it stuck in my brain. Please help us out of this mess, Lord. Don't let anything scary happen." She squeezed Erin's hand, and Erin prayed next.

"Father God, I'm sorry that I disobeyed, too. I don't know what verse Tess is talking about, but I know to obey. Please help us get back to the hotel, and don't let our moms be too worried. Thanks. Amen."

The girls lifted their heads, looking at one another with the first smile in an hour.

"Well, we're still here," Erin said. "What should we do?"

"I don't know." Tess bit her lip. She kicked her foot in the gravel, sending up a little cloud of dusty smoke. "Do you know what this reminds me of?"

"No. A mystery trip to an active volcano?" Erin asked. "Life in prison?"

"No." Tess giggled. "It reminds me of those sharks."

"What do you mean?" Erin pulled down her sweatshirt's sleeves, covering the field of goose bumps growing on her arms.

"At Sea World. You know, those baby sharks were so cute. And they didn't look harmful. But when they grow up, they're mean and dangerous. It's like my idea. It seemed good, you know, saving everybody time and finding something for Tyler." Tess blinked back tears. "But it grew into something mean and dangerous."

Erin scooted next to her friend. "Don't worry. Another bus will come."

"But when?" Tess said. "My mom will be so worried. And what if a bad guy comes first?" If something awful happened to her, it might just shock her mother enough that it could hurt her and the baby. Why did Tess think she could make these decisions on her own?

As she thought, a large, broadly built man strode around the corner from the military base and headed directly toward the bus bench. He wore a green and brown camouflaged uniform, like Tyler's G.I. Joe.

"I hope this one is a good guy, " Erin said.

"He's a soldier or sailor or something. I think he is," Tess answered. "Maybe he's our answer to prayer."

sixteen

MP to the Rescue

Thursday Evening, March 27

The man walked right by the girls, then stopped. And turned around.

"May I help you young ladies with something?" His big voice boomed through the silent night like thunder in the desert.

"Uh, maybe," Tess squeaked out. She licked her lips and willed some words from her parched mouth. "Actually, we're sort of lost. I mean, we are lost."

There. She had said it. Would he be helpful, or would he hurt them? She wasn't supposed to talk to strangers, but this one was a soldier, so it was okay. Or had she just broken another rule?

"Where are you going?" he asked, his voice softer this time.

"We're staying at the Hotel del Coronado," Erin spoke up. "Is there a phone around here?"

"As a matter of fact, there is. If you ladies would like to follow me to the guardhouse, I'll let you use it."

Erin looked at Tess, and Tess looked at Erin. Neither moved.

The man pointed to the patch on his shoulder. It read, "MP."

"I'm a Military Policeman," he said. "It's all right. But if you would rather, you can tell me your names, and I'll call your parents myself."

Exhaling loudly, Tess smiled. "Yes, that would be better. We could wait here if you would call my mother and ask her to come pick us up. Our name is Thomas."

The MP smiled, and the girls smiled back at him. "You'll be safe at this bus stop until they get here," he said. "No trouble happens right in front of the base." With that, he replaced the starched military cap on his head and walked toward the guard gate Tess had noticed.

"Well, it looks like our troubles are over!" Erin said.

"No, they're just beginning," Tess said. "Wait till my mother gets here. You ever hear of an Irish temper? Now you get to see one in real life." She kicked the gravel again, stirring up the dust. Night slipped completely over the sky, and the waves lapped against the shore, regular rhythms sounding more peaceful than she felt. Erin scooted closer to her on the bench. Sitting in stillness, it seemed like fewer than ten minutes before the Jeep screeched up, breaking the silence into a million pieces.

Mrs. Thomas leaped out of the car and raced toward Tess and Erin. Gathering them in a big bear hug, she squeezed them both, tears streaming down her cheeks.

"I'm so glad you're all right!" she cried.

"You are?" asked Tess. Maybe there wouldn't be trouble after all.

"Yes. Now that I know you're both okay, I can kill you myself!" Mrs. Thomas smiled, but Tess saw the tightened face muscles, too. Trouble was dead ahead.

The girls climbed into the car, and Tess saw Erin struggle not to cry. "Where's my mother?" she asked.

"In bed. She's not any better, and worrying her heart sick over you two didn't help. When the MP called and said you two were all right, it was all I could do to convince her to stay in bed." Mrs. Thomas jammed the Jeep into gear and lurched back onto the slim slip of highway running back to the hotel. Tess buckled in, as did Erin. Now that the ordeal was over, Tess started to cry.

"I'm…I'm sorry, Mom," she sobbed out. "I didn't mean to get us lost."

"Would someone like to explain to me what happened?" her mother said. She spoke quietly, but the stress in her voice was like a caged tiger, pacing the floor, waiting to roar forth.

"Well, we—I mean I—tried to find something for Tyler at the hotel shops. But there wasn't anything, and I really wanted to find him something special," Tess started, hoping to convince. She sniffed a little and continued.

"So I thought if we walked on Orange Avenue for a while maybe I would find something for him and then we could go back later and buy it. You know, so I wasn't dragging you and Mrs. Janssen around all day."

Mrs. Thomas broke in. "So you deliberately disobeyed me and did what you thought was best."

It didn't sound so good when her mother said it that way. "I guess so."

"How did you end up at a military post miles from town?" The tiger was pacing faster now, and her mom's voice rose.

"Well, we noticed it was getting late so we hopped on a

bus. So we could get back in time and not worry you," Tess added, hoping it would soften things.

"You mean so you wouldn't get in trouble," her mother corrected in a much louder voice.

Tess silently prayed, *Please, God, don't let my mother completely wig out in front of Erin.*

"Well, that too," she admitted aloud. She looked at Erin, who was shrinking as far back in her seat as she could. Tears crept into the corners of Erin's eyes, and Tess shook her head sadly. So much for being a Holiday Hero. Erin probably wished she never had come on this trip.

"So then we weren't looking out the window for just a second, I promise, and we rode past the hotel. By the time we noticed it we were right about" —she looked out the window— "where we are now. And then we didn't know what to do."

"Go on," her mother's voice was tight, ready to snap. Oh-oh.

"So we pulled the cord and got off at the first stop. Then we prayed together, and then the MP found us. But we didn't go with him. Wasn't that a good decision?" she asked, forcing a brightness into her voice.

"It was good to have him call," her mother admitted. "But *what were you thinking?*" she shouted.

Tess started to answer.

"No, don't answer that," her mother interrupted. "I don't want to know. At least not now. I need to simmer down and think about this for a while."

Tess knew the tiger was loose now, and she kept quiet. But her mother didn't. "Nancy and I were beside ourselves, worried sick. She has a terrible case of the flu, and this probably set her back days."

Erin muffled a sob.

"And as for Tyler, what kind of gift would it be to come home without you because you had been kidnapped or drowned?"

Tess didn't answer that it hadn't happened and that they hadn't gone near the water. It wouldn't have helped.

Mrs. Thomas swung the Jeep into the hotel parking lot and shut the engine off. "We prayed and prayed for at least fifteen minutes together, there on the bed, pleading for your safety."

Erin stopped sniffing, and Tess looked at her Secret Sister out of the corner of her eye. She didn't dare raise her head.

They had prayed together. As far as Tess knew, her mother never had prayed before. Tess held back a smile, not wanting to anger her mother further.

Thanks, Lord, she said inside her head. *You made something good from this.*

"We'll talk about this more in the room. And I'll have to think long and hard before we go to the beach-light marshmallow roast tonight."

The marshmallow roast! Tess had almost forgotten. She had sort of hoped to see the boys there. What if she had to miss it? And what if Erin's mom was really, really sick with worry?

seventeen

More Confession

Thursday Evening, March 27

They walked through the deserted parking lot and up the carpeted stairway toward their room. The night air smelled of sea salt and was thick with the perfume of the blossoms on Orange Avenue. Tess's mother wasn't taking time to enjoy any of that though. She strode ahead while Tess and Erin followed behind like two whipped dogs.

"C'mon, girls, I want to check on Nancy," Mrs. Thomas called over her shoulder. They passed the beautiful plants blooming in the courtyard, the smooth beige concrete tiles, the large sculptured ashtray with "Hotel del Coronado" stamped in the sand. Then they opened the door to their room.

"Mom!" Erin rushed past Tess and her mother, flying to the bed where her mother lay.

"Erin!" Her mother sat up, flinging back the layers of sheets and covers, to stand in a thin nightgown on wobbly legs. But her face had more color, and Tess thought she looked better. Whew. She was getting better, not worse.

Tess and her mother hung back, wanting to give Erin and her mom a little space. The two of them hugged for a minute; then Mrs. Janssen sat back down asking, "What happened?" Tess didn't think Erin's mom looked any happier than her own mother had.

The phone rang, and Mrs. Thomas answered it. Erin retold the account of their shopping trip and the bus ride down Orange Avenue, but Tess wasn't concentrating on her. Instead she held up her mother's plaque, the award she had won today. *I hope I didn't spoil her day*, Tess thought, her heart failing again.

When Erin finished telling about their day, she sat sniffing on the bed and snatched a tissue out of the box next to the clock.

"Oh, Erin, I'm so disappointed," her mother said. "What got into you?"

Tess didn't want to butt in, but she wanted to rescue Erin. "It was my fault, Mrs. Janssen. I wanted to look for something for Tyler, and I pretty much made all the decisions."

Erin's mother didn't say anything. She looked first at Erin, then at Tess. Silent. *Oh great. What if Erin's mom doesn't want Erin to be friends with me anymore?*

Finally Mrs. Janssen spoke. "Well, I don't see any handcuffs on Erin. She could have said no. But I'm disappointed in both of you."

Tess hung her head.

Just then her mother ended her phone conversation. "That was the vice president of advertising for the shoe firm. He wants me to stop by the beach house on the way to the marshmallow roast. And he said he would like to meet my daughter. So I guess you're going, even though I wasn't planning on it." Mrs. Thomas took a sip of water before continuing. "I wasn't about to tell him my daughter couldn't come because she had hopped a bus to Mexico."

At that, all four of them looked at each other. Tess's mom started to laugh first. Then Tess joined in. She got up to go to the bathroom, but before she reached the door, Erin and her mother were laughing, too. Erin flopped back on her mother's bed.

Tess chuckled all the way back from the bathroom a minute later. "Why are we laughing?" she asked, wiping her eyes.

"I don't know. Because we know you guys are safe, and I know you realize it was a bad thing to do. I guess it's funny to imagine you on the bus," Tess's mom said.

"Ha-ha, it wasn't very funny to be there," Erin said. But she giggled.

"I'll bet not!" her mother agreed.

Mrs. Thomas said, "Well, you girls had better change. If it's all right with you that Erin goes, too." She looked at Mrs. Janssen.

"It's okay," she agreed. Erin grabbed a new shirt and her jacket from the closet and took them into the bathroom with her. She called out, "Are you sure, Mom? Are you sure you're okay? 'Cause I can stay here."

"Actually, Erin, my fever is down, and I am feeling better. I think the worst is over. I even ordered some room service once I knew you girls were all right." She smiled.

Tess walked over to the drawer where she had stashed her shirts and dug through them till she found her Arizona State University sweatshirt. She pulled off her shirt, damp from the night and from nervousness, and pulled the sweat-shirt over her head. Then she dug in another drawer for a clean pair of socks.

"Hey, here's the last envelope from Tyler," she said.

"Well, read it." Erin opened the bathroom door while she rebraided her hair. Both mothers sat still as well. Maybe they liked these as much as Tess did.

"Okay, it says, 'WHEN IS THE FIRST TIME MEDICINE IS MEN-TIONED IN THE BIBLE?'"

"I give up," Erin called out.

"WHEN MOSES TOOK THE TWO TABLETS ON MT. SINAI!" Tess read. Her face screwed up in confusion. She asked, "Which tablets were those?"

"The Ten Commandments. Remember? He brought down the Ten Commandments that God had written on two tablets of stone." Erin came out of the bathroom, still applying her lip gloss.

"Oh yeah," Tess said. "I get it." Funny Tyler would think of that. Her whole family thought she was "religious" now that she went to Sunday school with Erin.

"One of those Ten Commandments is, 'Honor your father and mother,'" Erin's mother said. "You girls should give more thought to that."

"Actually," Tess said, "this is really weird, but that's part of the verse I've been thinking about this week."

"Oh?" her mother asked. Tess glanced at her. Her mother had never shown any interest in Tess's Bible reading before. Maybe that prayer had done something in Mrs. Thomas's heart, too.

Tess pushed on. "Want me to read it?"

"All right," her mother said. "I'm going to change in the bathroom. But I'll be listening through the door."

Tess thumbed through her Bible until she reached Ephesians, where she had stuck one of Tyler's cards. "It says, 'Children, obey your parents the way the Lord wants. This is the right thing to do. The command says, "Honor your father and mother." This is the first command that has a promise with it. The promise is: "Then everything will be well with you, and you will have a long life on the earth."'"

She closed the Bible and waited until her mother opened the bathroom door. "Do you think that seems wise?" her mom asked.

"Well, yes," Tess answered.

"Tyler disobeyed, and he almost got killed by a car. You disobeyed and got lost. You could have been hurt or much worse."

"I know," Tess said. "It didn't seem like that at the time though."

Her mother put her arm around Tess. "It never does. This isn't the last time we'll talk about it, but you've been so good the rest of the trip. I want you to know I appreciate that, too."

Tess gulped down the big lump of guilt sticking in her throat. What about the gondola ride? She glanced over at Erin, and Erin looked back at her. They were thinking the same thing.

Well, she had better confess. Maybe if she did it on the porch Mom wouldn't flip out as much, with the rest of the hotel guests listening. At least it wouldn't be in front of Erin and her mother.

"Actually, Mom, could we go out on the porch? There's something else I need to tell you."

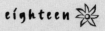

eighteen

Porch Talk

Thursday Night, March 27

Once they were out on the porch, Tess didn't know how to start. So much pressure and worry built up in her head that her eyeballs felt as if they would pop out.

"What is it, Tess?" her mother asked.

"Well, I want to be totally honest with you. And when you said I'd been good the rest of the trip, well, that's not exactly true."

Tess and her mother rocked back and forth in the white wicker chairs, side by side, gently keeping time with the ocean's rhythm. Neither looked at the other, staring instead at the kids playing tennis on the lighted court just beyond their room.

Her mom's silence was as thick as the stars scattered across the night sky. And probably just as hot, too.

Tess swallowed. "You know how you told us to sit down in the gondola at the zoo? I, uh, couldn't really see the gorillas when I was sitting down. You know how interesting they are…" Tess's voice trailed off.

Her mom stopped rocking. "And?"

"And so I stood up to see them better. Then the cart rocked, and I slammed my wrist on it."

Her mother lifted Tess's wrist and examined it.

"No, I didn't hurt it," Tess explained. "But my bracelet almost fell to the ground. I saved it though."

"Tess, forget about the bracelet falling. You could have fallen out of the gondola and been killed!"

"I know, Mom, I know. Believe me, I sat down the whole way back." She held her breath, waiting for her mom to explode. But she didn't. Tess bit her lip and looked toward the ground.

Her mother put her hand under Tess's chin and gently raised her face to eye level. "I'm going to tell you a story about when I was twelve," her mother said.

Tess sat back in her chair. This was not the way her mother usually handled discipline. But anything was better than having her freak out in public. Tess breathed a little deeper and slower now.

"When I was twelve, my best friend, Donna, and I wanted to buy some blue eye shadow. My mom didn't allow me to wear makeup, so I knew she would never give me the money, and I didn't have any saved up." Mrs. Thomas looked right at Tess.

Funny, Tess had never thought of her mom as having best friends. Or about her being twelve.

Her mother continued. "I knew my dad kept a big jar of change on top of his dresser. He put his pocket change in there every night. So one day I sneaked into his room and plucked four quarters from that jar. In my heart, I knew it was stealing, but I told myself it was their fault for being so strict. If they had just let me have some makeup, I wouldn't have to take the dollar. Donna and I bought the eye shadow, and it was neat for a while. But then it wasn't enough."

Tess stared at her mother. *Mom had stolen money?*

"So then," her mother continued, "I decided I needed some lipstick to go with it. The next week I crept back into my parents' room and put my hand into the jar again. This time I planned to take maybe two dollars so I could buy an eyelash curler, too. Do you know what happened next?"

"You got caught?"

"Yes, I got caught. My father walked into the room and saw me stealing those quarters. I wanted to die right then or run away from home. But I knew I couldn't."

"What happened?" Tess asked, a little breathless now.

"I got in big trouble. I wasn't allowed to play with Donna anymore, and I was grounded for a month. But my dad sat me down and looked me in the eye and told me, 'Molly, the first dollar is the hardest to steal.' Do you understand what he meant?"

"I guess that after you steal once it's easier to steal the next time."

"Yes. And he was right. The same is true with disobeying. Your disobeying once, on the gondola, made it easier to disobey on Orange Avenue. Do you understand?"

"I do," Tess said. And she did. But one terrible thought crossed her mind.

"Did you ever spend time with Donna again?"

"No."

Oh no! "Does that mean...does that mean that Erin and I

can't be best friends anymore?" *Please, God, don't let her say I can't have my Secret Sister.*

"You can still be friends." Her mother smiled. "Donna had other problems, and Erin is a very nice girl. But you can't go anywhere alone together for a while."

"Okay." Tess's heart softened. That did seem fair, after all.

Her mother stood up and stretched, holding her hand against the small of her back. "We had better get going to that marshmallow roast."

"Right!" Tess said.

After making sure Mrs. Janssen was comfortable, the three of them headed toward the beach. The night was calm now; the waves rippled in the distance. Even the hotel was quiet. Soft conversation drifted from a few open windows, and the gentle strumming of evening music in the Palm Court wafted over them.

"I'm going to stop in the beach house for just a minute," Tess's mother said. The beach house, a large white clapboard cottage on the edge of the beach, was a short walk from the main hotel. Surrounded by grapevines and blooming azaleas, it looked like a mini-palace from the South Seas.

"Did you know Marilyn Monroe stayed there?" Erin asked.

"Really?" Mrs. Thomas said. "How do you know?"

"I read it in the shopping gallery," Erin said. "Wouldn't it be fun to stay there?"

"It is nice," Mrs. Thomas admitted, "but a little too expensive for us. You girls don't need to come in. Just wait for me on the berm next to the beach." She pointed to an area about twenty feet away. "Do *not* go down to the beach without me. Stay glued! Then we'll all go down to the roast together."

"We will, Mom," Tess said. "You can count on us!"

She and Erin rambled over to the berm and stared at the water licking the salty shore. Little swirls of sea foam rolled up on the shore, then curled back under themselves and headed back out to sea. A lonely sea gull strutted across the sand, pecking here and there at empty mussel shells, looking for a bedtime snack.

"Isn't it dreamy to be at the beach?" Erin asked.

"Yeah. Are you still glad you came on this trip?" Tess asked. "Even with all the trouble we got into?"

"Of course I am! You're still my Holiday Hero. I mean, I'm sorry we got into some trouble, but mostly we had a lot of fun. And my mom isn't even very mad at me anymore." Erin hugged Tess, and Tess felt something brush against her shoulder as Erin enfolded her.

"What's that?" she asked.

"My candy bag," Erin said. Tess laughed. *Of course!*

"Do you want some?" Erin plucked out a piece of black sour licorice sprinkled with sugar crystals and bit off one end. The she sat down on the berm.

"No thanks. I think I'll wait for the marshmallows," Tess said. Bending over, she looked carefully at the green plants spreading across the berm. What did they grow on? She didn't see any dirt around them. Their thick green stems were like pea pods, and every couple of inches they cradled a thistle-colored blossom.

"I wonder what these are?" she said aloud.

"They're ice plants," Erin said, biting off another piece of licorice.

"What are you, a plant expert now?" Tess said.

"No, I read the sign next to the plants down the beach," Erin said. Tess stood up, stretching.

What was that? Out of the corner of her eye, a small shadow crept beside her, then over the berm toward the beach.

Was it a dog? No, it was the redhead and his weird friend skulking around. They headed toward the beach.

"Erin," Tess whispered, "look who's heading toward the water."

Erin jumped to her feet. "Are they smiling, or are they going to spoil the marshmallow roast?"

"I don't know."

Just then the two boys turned toward Tess and Erin.

"Look who it is," they called. And to Tess's horror, they started walking directly toward the girls.

nineteen

Rescue!

Thursday Night, March 27

"Hi, girls." The boys came right up and sat down next to Tess and Erin.

"What do you want?" Tess asked.

"Boy, you're not very friendly," the red-haired one said. But he smiled at Tess as he said it.

Tess looked at Erin, who looked back at her with wide eyes.

He continued. "We wanted to thank you for not tattling on us about switching the doorplates. So we're inviting you to beach comb with us before the marshmallow roast starts."

"You're going?" Tess asked.

"Yeah. My name is Danny. My dad works for the shoe company." The redhead smiled at her. "Does yours?"

"My mom writes advertising copy for them," Tess answered. The redhead was sort of nice after all. And they did have something in common.

"My name is Jack," the other one said. He sat next to Erin. "Want to see what I found?" He opened up his hand. In it lay a smooth, gray circle of shell, perfect swirls of rainbowed pearl covering the inside of it like cream sticking to a chocolate cookie.

"Oh, how beautiful," Erin said. "That must be why my mom wanted to go beach combing." She frowned. "Before she got sick, that is."

"You can hold it, if you want." He placed it in her hand, and she ran her fingers over the polished surface.

"Are there any others?" Erin asked.

"Yeah," Jack answered. "Tons. And some of them have pearls inside. That's why we came to get you guys. Do you want to come down and find them with us before the tide comes in?"

Children obey your parents…. Then everything will be well with you. Children obey your parents…. Then everything will be well with you. Those words circulated through Tess's head around and around, like a scratched CD.

She looked at Erin, and Erin looked at her and at the smooth, beautiful shell in Jack's hand.

twenty

Holiday Hero

Thursday Night, March 27

Without a doubt, the girls knew what their answer would be. "No way!" they both said at once.

"Why not?" The boys looked a little hurt.

"Well, we're not supposed to go on the beach without my mom," Tess said.

"Don't be such a goody-goody. You'll probably be back before your mom even comes," Danny said.

"Yeah, and wouldn't you like to find some shells for your mom?" Jack asked Erin.

"Well, yes," Erin wavered, looking at the beautiful pearly shell. Tess knew she was thinking of her sick mom, who hadn't had such a good day.

"I don't think she would want you to go on the beach to get it," Tess reminded her.

Erin looked back at Tess. "I guess you're right," she said. "Sorry, but thanks for asking."

Jack shrugged and pocketed the shell. "Suit yourself. I hope all the good ones aren't gone by the time your mom arrives."

With that, the two of them scrambled back down the berm and headed toward the beach.

"Well, it looks like we won't have long to wait," Tess said. "Here comes my mom now."

Mrs. Thomas strolled up with a man and paused and looked around for Tess. "Oh, there she is."

She walked up to the girls. "Tess, I'd like you to meet Mr. Elmer. He's the one I work with on the advertisements."

Mr. Elmer had shiny shoes and slicked back red hair. "Glad to meet you, young lady." He stuck out his hand. Tess offered hers. She had never really shaken hands before, but it looked like she was supposed to.

"How old are you?" he asked.

"Twelve," Tess answered.

"Hmm. My son, Dan, is twelve. He's here this week also. Too bad we didn't meet before. You might have enjoyed his company. He's here with his cousin Jack."

Tess's eyes grew large, and she swallowed fast to keep from laughing. This was Danny's dad?

"This is Tess's friend, Erin." Tess's mother jumped in before either of the girls could speak.

"Nice to meet you." Erin stuck out her hand.

"Same here," Mr. Elmer said. "Well, ladies, it's been nice, but I'd better go find my wife and head on down to the marsh-mallow roast." He turned to Mrs. Thomas. "Good work. Con-gratulations on the award. We'll look forward to seeing more of your ad pieces in the future." Then he turned to leave.

Mrs. Thomas blushed. "Well, I guess this trip was a suc-cess in spite of several, ah, problems."

They walked down to the beach, arm in arm. And Tess

didn't even feel geeky. She was glad to have both her mom and Erin close. The night surf continued to roll up the beach, sputtering pebbles and shell pieces, leaving them behind on the shore.

"Let's pick some up for your mom," Tess said. "Since she couldn't come down tonight."

"You two go ahead. Just don't walk off too far," Mrs. Thomas said.

Taking off their shoes and rolling up their pant legs, the girls wandered up and down the stretch of sand. They found a few cute shells, but none as nice as Jack's.

The waves washed over Tess's ankles, and the cool water soothed her. After pocketing a bunch of shells, she sat down with her mom and Erin on the dry sand to roast marshmallows.

"I'll roast them if you get us some s'more stuff," Erin said to Tess, skewering three marshmallows on one smooth birch stick.

Tess ran back to the table where the shoe company had provided food. She grabbed six graham crackers and some chocolate and met them back at the bonfire.

"Well, now we have your mom's souvenir," Mrs. Thomas said before biting into her gooey s'more. "And I have the caricatures."

"What about Tyler?" Tess wailed. "I feel so bad. I know I shouldn't have disobeyed, but I really did it for Tyler. I wanted to buy him something great. And now he has nothing. I don't think I can go home." She was almost crying.

Her mom smiled gently. "Well, I haven't had a chance to tell you with all the—ahem—excitement, today. But I got home from the awards ceremony a little early, so I called the zoo. They said we can stop in at the gift shop tomorrow on the way home." Her eyes twinkled. "They even have a stuffed horned lizard, a movie on reptiles, and a giant lizard photo book. So you'll have plenty to choose from."

"Oh, thank you, Mom!" Tess said. She should have known her mom would come up with something.

The stars twinkled in the sky. The winking points of light shimmered on the blurry mirror of water.

"Well, I guess that just leaves you," her mother said. "And Erin."

"Oh, I don't need a souvenir," Erin said. "This was the best trip ever. I'll carry it in my memory forever."

"Well, just in case you change your mind, your mother and I bought something for you girls." Mrs. Thomas handed a small, pearl-colored box to each girl. They opened them at the same time.

"Oh, Mom! Dolphin charms! Where did you find them?"

"At Sea World. Actually, Erin's mom found them when we went to buy the cotton candy. So she gets a big thanks, too."

"She will," Erin breathed. She clasped the charm on her bracelet, and Tess did the same. The silver glistened in the orange firelight. Then, as if thinking exactly the same thing at exactly the same time, the girls unclasped their bracelets and switched them.

"Secret Sisters forever?" Tess said, fastening Erin's bracelet on her arm.

"Forever," Erin agreed, fastening Tess's bracelet on her arm in return.

"And now," Mrs. Thomas said, "I want another s'more."

"Me, too," Erin said.

Tess smiled indulgently. "I'll wait here."

After they had gone to bring back the s'more ingredients, Tess looked at the sparkling sky. "Thank you, Lord, for protecting me and Erin and Tyler. And especially for this trip. I don't care what Erin says, I know the truth. You are the real Holiday Hero."

She looked from side to side to make sure no one was watching her; then she blew a kiss toward heaven.

Have More Fun!!

Visit the official website at:
www.secretsisters.com

There are lots of activities, exciting contests, and a chance for YOU to tell me what you'd like to see in future Secret Sisters books! AND—be the first to know when the next Secret Sisters book will be at your bookstore by signing up for the instant e-mail update list. See you there today!

If you don't have access to the Internet, please write to me at:

> Sandra Byrd
> P.O. Box 2115
> Gresham, OR 97030

Secret Note Stashes

This trip, Tess's brother was left behind, but he sent along some notes to help her have fun without him. Next time you or your Secret Sister goes on a trip, why not exchange a note stash?

For each day you'll be apart, write your Secret Sister a note. Include a joke or two, tell her that you're thinking about her, and promise that you'll get her some cool postcards and a trinket (or remind her to get one for you)! Be sure to think up some fun things you'll do together later on. Choose a different color paper for each day, and decorate with stamps or stickers.

❀ **Is the wedding on? Well, don't be late. Solve these clues, then read Book Eight!**

Across

3 A vacation that follows a wedding

6 Woman or girl who stands with the bride at a wedding

7 When you go into the hospital for surgery, you're having an _____.

8 If you envy someone else's success, you're _____.

10 Terrible trouble

11 You got into trouble, and now you can't talk on the phone or go anywhere. You're _____.

12 Beautiful blossoms that grow mostly in spring and summer

Down

1 The opposite of the truth is a _____.

2 A place you go to work and earn money

3 Meat patties on buns with ketchup and mustard

4 A ceremony in which a man and woman are married

5 Tess's teacher's last name

9 Something unexpected; a wonderful _____.

Look for the Other Titles in
Sandra Byrd's Secret Sisters Series!
Available at your local Christian bookstore

Available Now:

#1 *Heart to Heart:* When the exclusive Coronado Club invites Tess Thomas to join, she thinks she'll do anything to belong—until she finds out just how much is required.

#2 *Twenty-One Ponies:* There are plenty of surprises—and problems—in store for Tess. But a Native American tale teaches her just how much God loves her.

#3 *Star Light:* Tess's mother becomes seriously ill, and Tess's new faith is tested. Can she trust God with the big things as well as the small?

#4 *Accidental Angel:* Tess and Erin have great plans for their craft-fair earnings. But after their first big fight will they still want to spend it together? And how does Tess become the "accidental" angel?

#5 *Double Dare:* A game of "truth or dare" leaves Tess feeling like she doesn't measure up. Will making the gymnastics team prove she can excel?

#6 *War Paint:* Tess must choose between running for Miss Coronado and entering the school mural painting contest with Erin. There are big opportunities—and a big blowout with the Coronado Club.

#7 *Holiday Hero:* This could be the best Spring Break ever—or the worst. Tess's brother, Tyler, is saved from disaster, but can the sisters rescue themselves from even bigger problems?

#8 *Petal Power:* Ms. Martinez is the most beautiful bride in the world, and the sisters are there to help her get married. When trouble strikes her honeymoon plans, Tess and Erin must find a way to help save them.

The Secret Sister Handbook: 101 Cool Ideas for You and Your Best Friend! It's fun to read about Tess and Erin and just as fun to do things with your own Secret Sister! This book is jam-packed with great things for you to do together all year long.